RAISING THE DEAD

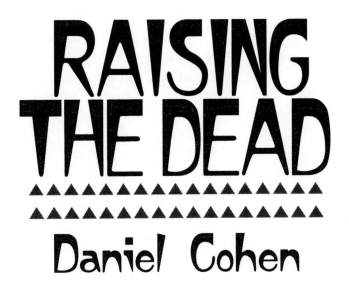

RAISING THE DEAD

▲▲▲▲▲▲▲▲▲▲▲▲▲▲▲▲▲▲▲▲
▲▲▲▲▲▲▲▲▲▲▲▲▲▲▲▲▲▲▲▲

Daniel Cohen

COBBLEHILL BOOKS

Dutton   New York

To Boris Karloff,
the greatest of them all

Library of Congress Cataloging-in-Publication Data
Cohen, Daniel, date
Raising the dead / Daniel Cohen.
p.   cm.
Includes bibliographical references and index.
ISBN 0-525-65255-8
1. Occultism.   2. Voodooism.   3. Zombiism.   4. Body Snatching.
5. Dead—Miscellanea.   I. Title.
BF1411.C62   1997
306.9—dc21   97-3135   CIP

Published in the United States by Cobblehill Books,
an affiliate of Dutton Children's Books,
a member of Penguin Putnam Inc.,
375 Hudson Street, New York, New York 10014

Designed by Mina Greenstein
Printed in the United States of America
First Edition   10 9 8 7 6 5 4 3 2 1

CONTENTS

INTRODUCTION

To the Grave and Beyond

I spent (or in the view of my parents and some of my teachers, misspent) a large part of my youth sitting in darkened movie theaters watching horror films or reading horror stories and novels.

As a result, my mind was, and still is, cluttered with images of gigantic half-alive creatures lumbering across the landscape; of mad scientists and their crazed assistants in laboratories crackling with electricity, and filled with bubbling chemicals; of graveyards where sinister-looking men dig up bodies and carry them off; and of mummies who guard their tombs with lethal efficiency.

I suspect that you're a lot like me or you would never have picked up a book like this in the first place. And like me, you have probably wondered, "Are these stories true?" Not literally true, perhaps; we know that movies and novels are fiction. But where did the ideas for the stories come from? Is there any truth behind them, or do they spring completely from the imaginations of novelists and screenwriters?

Well, that's what this book is about.

In previous books I have examined the facts and legends behind two of the great figures of horror—the vampire and the werewolf. In this book we're going to look at some of the other great figures in the pantheon of horror—the monster as in the Frankenstein monster, the mummy, and the zombie. We're also going to look at some lesser-known monsters like the golem and an assortment of magicians and mad scientists who either try to bring things back to life, or try to keep themselves alive long after they should have been dead and buried. Then there are the body snatchers, the grave robbers without whom no mad scientist could really do his job. These are the boys who, in the words of a gruesome little children's rhyme, supply "the beef."

And finally, there are those bodies which while undoubtedly dead, have certainly not been buried.

It's all you ever wanted to know about the undead, the near dead, and the unburied.

1
▼ ▼

The Monster

"It's alive! It's alive!"

We all know what Dr. Frankenstein's creation looks like. He's like an old friend. He's more familiar to us than George Washington or Babe Ruth.

He's Boris Karloff with a square head, big stitches, greenish skin, and electronic connectors sticking out of his neck. He's a tall, lurching figure in shabby, ill-fitting clothes and huge boots.

And we all know how the monster was brought to life. He was assembled from body parts stolen from graveyards, and then subjected to huge jolts of electricity from a thunderstorm raging outside of the castle laboratory. Then as the dead hand, visible from underneath the sheet, begins to twitch convulsively,

Dr. Henry Frankenstein, a thin, borderline hysteric, begins to shout, "It's alive! It's alive!"

What has been described here are scenes from the 1931 film *Frankenstein*, probably the best-known horror film ever made. None of this—none of it—appears in the novel, first published over a century earlier, which inspired this film and so many other adaptations.

You may think you know Frankenstein, but you don't. In the film even the doctor's name was, for some unaccountable reason, changed from Victor to Henry, though it became Victor again in most later Frankenstein films.

The biggest difference is that in the film the monster is mute—aside from an occasional grunt or whimper. In the novel the monster talks—and talks, and talks, about himself and his plight, and how miserable he feels, and the modern reader feels like shouting, "Shut up already!"

The novel *Frankenstein* isn't even a horror story in the usual sense. It's a good old-fashioned gothic romance, of the type that is not often read today. There is much turning pale, clutching at the throat, and swooning. Have you ever read the novel *Frankenstein* all the way through? Do you know anyone who has? I'll bet not.

And yet it is a book that began inspiring plays almost from the moment it was published. It is one of the very first books ever made into a film and has been adapted for films more often than any other single work of fiction. When you talk about raising the dead, Frankenstein is the first name that comes to mind. The book must have something. And indeed it does.

Frankenstein, for all its dated wordiness, is a remarkable work. One reason is that it was written by an eighteen-year-old girl. Of course, Mary Shelley wasn't your average eighteen-year-old girl. She was the daughter of William Godwin, a radical intellectual and writer, and Mary Wollstonecraft, also a radical writer, and one who is far better known than her husband. Her book, *A Vindication of the Rights of Women*, published in 1792, made her famous and is still regarded as one of the basic documents of the women's movement today.

But Mary Wollstonecraft died from complications in the birth of her daughter, so the creator of *Frankenstein* never knew her brilliant and celebrated mother, though she certainly knew about her and adopted the name Wollstonecraft.

At the age of seventeen, Mary met and fell in love with the poet, Percy Bysshe Shelley. Shelley returned the feeling, but there was a problem—the poet was already married and had two children. As radical and artistic people, they felt themselves above the conventional morality of the time, and on July 28, 1814, the couple ran off together to the European continent. When they returned to England, they were beset by a whole host of troubles, particularly by the social pressures that the English gentry reserved for lovers they considered sinful.

So, in 1816, the couple left England again and made their way across Europe to Switzerland where they rented a house on the shores of Lake Leman. Nearby was a villa occupied by an even more famous and notorious English poet, Lord Byron. The result came to be called "The *Frankenstein* Summer."

Byron was accompanied by his personal physician, John Polidori. The two households met frequently for sailing around the lake and picnics. They were a young group. Byron, the oldest, was twenty-eight; Shelley was twenty-three; Mary, eighteen; Polidori, twenty-one.

It was a rainy summer in Switzerland that year, and the group had to spend a lot of time indoors where they were getting bored and depressed. They had all been reading and discussing an English translation of a collection of German horror tales that had come their way.

Then one evening, according to Mary's later account, Byron made a suggestion:

" 'We will each write a ghost story,' said Lord Byron, and his proposition was acceded to. There were four of us."

Byron himself never got beyond writing a fragment of a story. Shelley, who was a poet and not a writer of stories, wrote something poetic about his early life. "Poor Polidori had some terrible idea about a skull-headed lady, who was so punished for peeping through a keyhole—what to see I forgot—something very shocking and wrong of course . . ."

A short time later, however, Polidori was to pick up on an idea that Byron had floated at the time, and produced the novel *The Vampyre.* It isn't a very good novel, but it was the first vampire novel written in English, and the elegant Lord Ruthven, the vampire in the story, became the model for the much more famous and elegant Count Dracula, and for all the elegant vampires of the Anne Rice novels.

Mary Shelley, the youngest of the company, came up with *Frankenstein.* If the weather had been better in Switzerland that summer, the entire course of horror fiction in English might have been very different.

So that's how the Frankenstein monster was really created. But it didn't all happen at once, in a blinding flash of inspiration. For several days Mary was able to do nothing with Byron's assignment. In the meantime, she sat by and listened as Byron and Shelley discussed various philosophical doctrines, "and among others the nature of the principle of life, and whether there was any probability of its ever being discovered and communicated."

6 :: Raising the Dead

That night she dreamed of: ". . . the pale student of unhallowed arts kneeling beside the thing he had put together. I saw the hideous phantasm of a man stretched out, and then . . ." That was the beginning.

She didn't sit down and write the book in a creative frenzy. It took her months of hard work and rewriting, and then months more before a publisher could be found for the work even though Shelley, who was well known in literary circles, pestered just about everyone he knew to get the book published. *Frankenstein* was finally published anonymously in March of 1818, by a not quite respectable publisher who specialized in sensational literature. Reviews were decidedly mixed, one reviewer calling it "a tissue of horrible and disgusting absurdity." Other reviews called it excellent, and when they found out that the book had actually been written by a woman, they found it quite remarkable. Women were not supposed to write, or even think like that.

Whatever the critics thought, the public seemed to like the book. It sold well and within a few years was made the basis for the first of many stage and later screen adaptations.

Mary Shelley's life was essentially a tragic one. Only one of her five children survived to adulthood. Percy Shelley himself, whom she married after his wife's death, was drowned in a boating accident in 1822. Mary Shelley wrote a number of other books after *Frankenstein*, but none of them was ever particularly successful. Yet with the continuing proceeds from *Frankenstein*, as well as what she had been able to earn from her other works, she and her son were able to live quite comfortably until her death in 1851.

The Victor Frankenstein of the novel is not the white-coated mad scientist of the films. He is a brilliant young college student who becomes obsessed with the ideas of alchemical philosophers and magicians like Cornelius Agrippa and Paracelsus. "I entered with greatest diligence into the search for the philosophers' stone and the elixir of life . . ." While such interests were considered out of date, and not quite respectable in Mary Shelley's day, they were not regarded as altogether loony either. In the films, Frankenstein was a baron, a nobleman, but in the novel he is the son of a respected and very respectable civil servant.

Victor Frankenstein carries out many of his researches in graveyards and burial vaults. Just exactly what he does is never described. All we are told is "A sudden light broke in upon me—a light so brilliant and wondrous, yet so simple, that while I became dizzy with the immensity of the prospect which it illustrated, I was surprised that among so many men of genius, who had directed their inquiries toward the same science, that I alone should be reserved to discover so astonishing a secret."

But as to what the "secret" might be we haven't a clue.

Of course, the inspiration was just the start. It took Victor months of hard work to complete his work. Again, details are lacking, but we can discern it was a dirty job. "The dissecting room and the slaughter-house furnished many of my materials; and often did my human nature turn with loathing from my occupation."

There was no castle, no huge laboratory, no de-formed assistant. Frankenstein's "workshop of filthy creation," as he called it, was "a solitary chamber, or rather cell, at the top of the house."

The process by which the creature is brought to life is not described at all, though electricity, which plays such a large part in the film, does not seem to have been involved. All we know is that ". . . on a dreary night of November, I beheld the accomplishment of my toils.

"I saw the dull yellow eye of the creature open; and a convulsived motion agitated its limbs."

Victor Frankenstein's creature is never described in any detail, but from the little we are told, we know it didn't look like Boris Karloff in full makeup.

"His limbs were in proportion, and I selected his features as beautiful. Beautiful!—Great God! His yel-lowish skin scarcely covered the work of muscles and arteries beneath; his hair was of a lustrous black, and

flowing; his teeth of pearly whiteness; but these lux-
uriances only formed a more horrid contrast with his
watery eyes that seemed almost the same colour as
the dun white sockets in which they were set, his
shriveled complexion and straight black lips." This,
and the fact that the creature is of larger than normal
size and strength, is just about all we do know about
its appearance. There is no flat skull, no electrical
connections in the neck.

When Bram Stocker sat down to write *Dracula* he
left a very full record of his researches, so that we
know that he based his vampire count on Vlad Tepes,
a particularly bloodthirsty fourteenth-century prince
of Transylvania. Mary Shelley was not so obliging,
and so we can only speculate whether there was a
"real" Frankenstein, an historical character on which
Shelley based her novel.

Actually, there were plenty of "real" Frankensteins
in Germany, and there still are. The name is a common one and some of the Frankensteins were barons.
There is a legend of how one of the early Barons
Frankenstein, Georg von Frankenstein, killed a monster, though in this case the monster was either a very
small dragon or a very large snake. There were the
ruins of a big gloomy Castle Frankenstein. In fact,
the name Frankenstein means "castle of the Franks."
The massive medieval fortress known as Castle
Frankenstein near the Rhine River looks as if it in-

spired Hollywood, and it probably did. But did it inspire Mary Shelley? We can't be sure, though she may have passed the area when she visited Europe during 1816.

None of the Barons Frankenstein were known to have any particular interest in alchemy, which was of great interest to the fictional Victor Frankenstein. There is, however, an alchemical connection to Castle Frankenstein, and quite an intriguing one at that. It is the brilliant and enigmatic man named Konrad Dippel.

Dippel was actually born at Castle Frankenstein on August 10, 1673, when his parents and a lot of other German refugees had flocked to the fortress to escape the armies of the French that were ravaging the countryside at that time.

Konrad was a strange, solitary, but highly intelligent boy who considered himself a "superior" individual animated by a "higher spirit," which gave him exceptional powers by which he could penetrate the mysteries of the universe. When he registered at the University, he used the name "Frankenstenia."

Konrad Dippel was trained as a theologian, a physician, and an alchemist—not an unusual combination for a scholar in those days. But because he had a quarrelsome nature, and was always questioning authority, he had a difficult time settling down anywhere, and took up the life of a wandering scholar and lecturer. He was considered a visionary who had the power of divination and prophecy by some of his students. Other people considered him a nuisance, a pest, and a menace to public order and morality. He was forced to flee from Strausberg, owing to a "serious incident" reportedly involving stealing bodies from a local cemetery.

Dippel moved back to the city of Darmstadt, near Castle Frankenstein where his parents lived, and plunged ever more deeply into the practice and study of alchemy. He frequently consulted the works of Cornelius Agrippa and Paracelsus, who were also favorites of Mary Shelley's fictional Victor Frankenstein. Dippel seems to have tried to purchase Castle Frankenstein itself as the ideal location for his alchemical experiments, but he couldn't afford it. Instead, he purchased a smaller property in the vicinity—planning to pay for it with the gold that he created through his alchemical experiments. Dippel claimed to have actually succeeded in making gold. However, there is a tradition that the alchemist must never use the gold he creates for personal gain. Dippel broke that rule by using the gold to buy a large estate. And then, according to legend, he accidentally broke the jar containing the "Philosophers' Stone" that he had worked so hard to achieve, and the secret was lost. In the lore of alchemy the Philosophers' Stone is the mysterious substance that can be used to transform lead into gold and also can confer immortality on the alchemist. Dippel was unable to repeat his discovery and after three years left Darmstadt and took up his life of wandering again.

Like many alchemists, Konrad Dippel was fascinated by the idea of creating life. He believed that the body was an inert substance that was animated by some sort of "vital spirit." Dippel thought that the creation of life simply meant facilitating the passage of a spirit into an inanimate corpse. Just how this was to be accomplished, however, was something he never made clear. Most probably he didn't know what to do, but simply assumed that it could be done.

Dippel kept up his travels throughout Europe for twenty-five years, at times attaining great success and wealth, at other times being thrown in jail. In Denmark, he received the title of "Royal Counselor" at one point. Shortly thereafter, he was sentenced to life imprisonment and all his books were publicly burned by the official hangman. He spent a very uncomfortable year in a small, damp cell in a castle on an island in the Baltic, but was released through the intervention of the Danish queen, and for a time became her personal physician.

In Sweden, Dippel was so popular that he was called "the Messiah of the nobility." He was also denounced as a Russian spy. In Germany, he had been called a Swedish spy. After an exciting, perhaps too exciting, quarter-century of wandering and sometimes running, Dippel returned to Germany and bought a house just a few miles from Castle Frankenstein. And he resumed his attempts to obtain the castle, but in a most unusual way.

Dippel claimed to have discovered certain unnamed alchemical "secrets." These he offered to give to the ruler of the area in return for Castle Frankenstein and its domains. He would assume the status of Lord of Frankenstein. Just what these "secrets" were is unknown; negotiations for the castle broke down, and nothing ever came of this transaction. An air of mystery surrounds the entire episode.

One possible clue to the nature of the "secrets" may come from a strange pamphlet that Dippel had printed in 1733, shortly after negotiations for the castle failed, and while his enemies were circulating rumors of his impending death. He announced that he had discovered the secret of prolonging his own life until the year 1801 when he would be 135 years old. That wasn't immortality, but it was an unprecedented life span then, and still is today.

Dippel was wrong. On the morning of April 24, 1724, about a year after he predicted that he would live until 1801, he was found dead in a room in the palace of his friend, Count Augustus von Wittgenstein. The cause of his death is a matter of controversy. Some thought he had died of apoplexy—what we would today call a stroke. Others believed he had been poisoned, either by his enemies or that the poison had been self-administered. A few said that he had been killed by the Devil for not keeping his contract. The alchemist's body was buried on Count Wittgenstein's land, but it disappeared, "trailed by the strangest rumors," says one authority.

Since Castle Frankenstein was so closely associated with the alchemist, some people got the idea that gold the alchemist created might be buried somewhere in or near the castle, which was at that time deserted. Over the next fifty years, bands of treasure seekers dug around, and hacked and even blasted away at the castle. They found nothing of interest, but several were killed by falling rocks or explosions during the excavations. Finally, local authorities enforced a strict ban on all further digging in the area.

By Mary Shelley's time the castle had become something of a tourist attraction for those who loved gloomy old ruins and the Gothic atmosphere. In recent times the castle has been restored and tourists can rent rooms in it.

It is unknown whether Mary Shelley actually visited Castle Frankenstein before 1816, or that she even knew about the alchemist Dippel, though he was certainly a well-known figure at the time. While the Victor Frankenstein of the novel was a noble if misguided character, Konrad Dippel was flamboyant, arrogant, and clearly something of a charlatan. But there are so many parallels between the life of the real Konrad Dippel and the Victor Frankenstein of the novel, that they seem more than coincidental.

In his book *In Search of Frankenstein*, the scholar Radu Florescu says of the pair: "Both were exceptional minds, far ahead of their times, little understood by their superiors and peers; both scientific Hamlets condemned to wander from country to country, even to suffer imprisonment because of their work. Both firmly believed in the ability of man to conquer death, and to create life by artificial means, and both worked in secrecy."

Konrad Dippel may indeed be the "real Frankenstein."

Dr. Frankenstein's monster first sprang to life on the stage in London in 1823, under the title *Presumption or the Fate of Frankenstein*. It created such a stir that the producers decided to tone down some of the horrors because scenes were frightening ladies in the audience.

They didn't frighten Mary Shelley when she went to see the production. "I was much amused," she wrote. "But lo and behold! I found myself famous. *Frankenstein* had prodigious success as a drama . . ."

Other stage versions were to follow, including parodies with names like *Frankenstich* and *Fank-n-*

Steam. But it was the films that truly made Mary Shelley's story part of our common culture.

Frankenstein films are nearly as old as films themselves. The first known film version was made by the Edison Company in 1910, practically the dawn of the movie industry. The film itself is now lost, but since it was only ten minutes long, it could not have been a very full version of the story. A surviving still from the film shows actor Charles Ogle made up as a hideous and very effective monster.

In 1915, there was another silent version called *Life Without a Soul*. This one ran a little under an hour and was quite successful. But *the* Frankenstein film was the Universal Pictures production in 1931. It followed on the heels of Universal's enormously successful production of *Dracula*. Bela Lugosi, who became a star in *Dracula*, was considered for the part of the monster, but he turned it down. He didn't think that a film in which he had no real lines would be good for his career. It was a decision that he was to sorely regret. The part was then given to a relatively unknown contract player named Boris Karloff. Karloff didn't even get full screen credit when the film first opened. The credits read "The Monster . . . ? ? ?" Of course it was no real secret who played the part and it made Karloff an immediate star, who soon eclipsed Lugosi in the horror field. The makeup was created by Universal's master makeup artist, Jack Pierce.

Karloff didn't look like the creature in Mary Shelley's book. The script didn't follow the original story at all. But it truly made Frankenstein's and Mary Shelley's creation of a creature, constructed from parts of the dead, immortal.

Usually once a film classic is made, the sequels tend to be disappointing. In this case the sequel *The Bride of Frankenstein*, released in 1935, is actually better than the original version, and it is closer in tone to the Mary Shelley novel. It starts with a scene in which Elsa Lanchester, who later plays the monstrous "bride," takes the part of Mary Shelley telling Shelley and Lord Byron the Frankenstein story—a recreation of sorts of the events of the summer of 1816. A lovely touch.

The idea of a "bride" for Frankenstein (actually, for the monster, but by this time the names of creator and created had become thoroughly confused in the mind of the public, and they still are), did not originate in Hollywood. In the novel the creature wants Frankenstein to create a "mate" for him, so that he will no longer be alone in the world. Frankenstein first agrees, but ultimately destroys his second creation before it can be brought to life. The consequences of this act are terrible.

This film introduces Dr. Praetorius, an evil magician/alchemist, wonderfully played by Ernest Thesiger, whose macabre theories on the creation of life are one of the film's many high points.

Bride was a huge success, though it is not seen as often today as the original film. It inspired yet another sequel, *Son of Frankenstein*, released in 1938. This film was Karloff's last outing as the monster in the movies. While it's not as good as the two earlier films, the quality is still remarkably high. Basil Rathbone plays the son, not of the monster but of Frankenstein. Bela Lugosi is there as the deformed assistant, Ygor, his best screen performance after Dracula. Lionel Atwell is the wooden-armed police chief. The sight of Atwell sticking darts into his wooden arm during one crucial scene is gallows humor at its best. These two characters are so good that they have become a permanent part of the Frankenstein legend. People think that they were in the original movie, or even in the book. But they weren't.

At this point, Karloff got tired of lugging around the cumbersome Frankenstein monster costume, which aggravated his already bad back. And he didn't like what the scriptwriters were doing to what he always called "my dear old monster." So he retired from playing the monster, though he did reprise it briefly in a television appearance. After *Son*, the quality of the Frankenstein films declined rapidly, until with *Abbott and Costello Meet Frankenstein*, the monster became more of a joke than a fright. The best horror film spoof of all times is Mel Brooks' *Young Frankenstein*.

Other studios and later, television, took the Frankenstein story, producing a flock of perfectly dreadful films, and a few pretty good ones, though no one has come close to the original Universal Pictures series.

All in all, one must conclude that the movies have been pretty good to Victor Frankenstein's and Mary Shelley's creation. They have indeed brought the creature back to life time after time and given it a kind of immortality.

2

▼▼ ▼

The Mummy's Curse

"Death comes on wings to he
who enters the tomb of a pharaoh."

That is supposed to be the mummy's curse, or the pharaoh's curse, or the curse of King Tut. It is, according to the popular legend, an inscription that was found in the tomb of King Tutankhamen, when the tomb was opened in 1922. And it is said that the curse has resulted in the death of many of those who had been involved in opening the tomb. People who know virtually nothing else about ancient Egypt or its mummies know about the curse, or think they do.

The story of the mummy's curse has been told so many times, in so many places by so many different people, that almost everyone assumes it's true. It's a good creepy story—but it isn't true. There is no mummy's curse and there never was.

Here's how the story began. The ancient Egyptians probably spent more time, energy, and treasure protecting the bodies of their dead, particularly their dead kings, than any other people in history. But the Egyptians relied more on heavy doors, concealed tombs, and guards to protect their mummies than they did on curses. In fact, in the voluminous records and tomb inscriptions of ancient Egypt that have survived, there is not a single tomb curse to be found.

About the closest thing to a curse found in any Egyptian tomb was an inscription in the tomb of the Fourth Dynasty courtier, Meni. It was a warning to anyone who had helped build the tomb and then complained he had not been paid. "I paid him for it," reads the inscription. "Let the crocodile be against him in the water, the snake against him on land. I have never done anything against him and it is the god who will judge him for it." In other words, Meni would do nothing against him and it was for the god alone to judge him.

Besides, if there really had been curses on tombs, they didn't work, and they certainly didn't scare anyone off. Countless generations of robbers made a very good living plundering tombs. In some areas of Egypt, tomb robbing was the family business. And the tomb robbing didn't begin centuries after people stopped believing in the old gods of Egypt either. Many tombs were plundered practically before the cement on the doors had dried. The robbers were often the very people who had been chosen to guard the tomb in the first place. While there is no record of ancient curses, there are ancient records of the trials of tomb robbers.

Since ancient Egyptian rulers and nobles insisted on being buried with many of their earthly goods, the lure of the buried wealth always overwhelmed any fear robbers may have had of retribution in this world or the next. As a result, every single royal tomb in Egypt had been thoroughly plundered in ancient times—except one.

In that great burial ground called the Valley of the Kings, the well-concealed tomb of an obscure, insignificant, and short-lived Eighteenth Dynasty king named Tutankhamen (nicknamed King Tut in modern times) had escaped the attention of the ancient tomb robbers. Perhaps he was so unimportant that he just slipped beneath their notice. Actually, the tomb's discoverers found there had been at least one attempt to plunder the tomb in ancient times, but for some unknown reason, the intruders only got into an outer chamber and never touched all the really valuable stuff inside.

However, King Tut's name had appeared on lists of kings, so twentieth-century archaeologists knew that his tomb must be out there somewhere. The trick was finding it.

In 1922, a British archaeologist named Howard

Carter did find the tomb, and along with his patron, Lord Carnarvon, who had financed the expedition, gained the glory of making the most spectacular and well-publicized archaeological discovery of the twentieth century.

Carter and Carnarvon also became the first people in some four thousand years to enter the inner precincts of the royal tomb.

In March, 1923, about six months after the tomb had been discovered the American occult novelist, Marie Corelli, wrote a letter to *The New York Times* stating that she had in her possession an early Arabic book about opening Egyptian tombs. She said the book stated that "Death comes on wings to he who enters the tomb of a pharaoh."

Just a few days later, Lord Carnarvon died in Cairo, from complications that developed out of an infected mosquito bite. The cause of death sounded so trivial that it seemed almost unnatural. Add to that, on the night Carnarvon died all the lights in Cairo suddenly went out!

The day the news of Carnarvon's death reached England, the *Times* of London was interviewing Sir Arthur Conan Doyle, the creator of Sherlock Holmes. By this time in his life, Sir Arthur had become a confirmed spiritualist, and he held all manner of other occult beliefs that his rigorously logical creation, Holmes, would have rejected as absurd. But Sir Arthur was a famous and influential man. The reporter mentioned the Corelli letter, and Sir Arthur said that he believed that the death had indeed been caused by an ancient curse. That statement made front-page news around the world—and so the legend of the mummy's curse was born.

The story continued to build for years. Every time someone connected with the opening of the tomb died, it was cited as proof that the dead pharaoh had again struck from beyond the grave. There was even a story that shortly before the tomb was opened a cobra, one of the symbols of Egyptian royalty, had eaten Carter's pet canary.

An attempted rational explanation of the curse was that some unknown but deadly ancient bacteria or virus, which had been sealed up inside the tomb, infected many of those who entered it and ultimately killed them.

Is there any significance in all the deaths that are supposed to have accompanied the opening of King Tut's tomb? Probably not. The most striking objection to the curse story is that Howard Carter, the man who actually discovered the tomb and the obvious first target for any curse, lived on for seventeen more years. If there was a curse at work, it wasn't working very swiftly. After the discovery, Carter spent most of his time fighting with Egyptian officials and others, cataloging and lecturing about his great find. He got so sick of answering questions about "the curse" that when the subject was mentioned, he would get very angry and refuse to talk about it. Many others who had been associated with the discovery and opening of the tomb lived normal, or even extremely long, lives. The list of those who died young or suddenly within a few years of the opening of the tomb is not unusually large, considering the huge number of people who were in one way or another associated with the discovery.

Lord Carnarvon's death is not as mysterious as it can be made to sound. He had been in poor health for years. He started going to Egypt in the first place in order to avoid the damp and cold British climate. Death, even from an apparently insignificant infection, was far more common in the pre-antibiotic days of 1923 than it is today. Carnarvon may have already had a damaged immune system before he got the infected mosquito bite.

How about that blackout in Cairo? Power failures were common in Cairo in 1923. In fact, they still are.

We don't know exactly were Marie Corelli got her "Death comes on wings . . ." curse. If it was from an early Arabic book, as she claimed, that would not have been a very good source. The Egypt of the pharaohs is extremely ancient, and long before the Arabs began writing about it, all contact with the dead civilization had been lost. The Arabs could no longer read the ancient hieroglyphics. Even if there actually had been a curse inscribed in some of the tombs, they wouldn't have known about it. The Arabs were just as fascinated and puzzled by the ancient Egyptians' strange and elaborate funerary rites as everyone else has been. Like many others, some Arabic writers assumed that the ancient Egyptians possessed all manner of mystic and magical secrets—but they hadn't a clue as to what these secrets might have been.

Today, we can read the ancient hieroglyphics and we have a much better idea as to what the ancients believed about death, but there are still gaps in our knowledge and there probably always will be. Ancient Egyptian civilization lasted for thousands of years, longer than any other civilization in human history. Egypt was also an extremely conservative society. The Egyptians never really abandoned old beliefs for new ones, they just added the new ones to the old ones. The end result was that their religious and magical ceremonies became incredibly complicated and to us, at least, they don't seem to make a lot of sense. We can read the words, but we are not sure of the inner meaning of the ceremonies.

For the Egyptians there was an afterlife, another world after death. The preservation of the body—the mummy—played an extremely important role in the passage of what we would call the soul of the dead person from this world to the next. Actually, the

Egyptians appeared to believe that each individual, or at least each royal or high-born individual, possessed several souls or spirits. Some made the journey to the next world—while others hovered about on earth near the tomb and the mummy. These beliefs are, as already mentioned, very confusing and alien to us. We ask, if the soul had gone to join the gods in the other world, why was it so vital to preserve and protect the body in this world? We only know that it was.

One thing that was very important to an Egyptian was that his "name" be remembered—that, in some way, helped to assure immortality. Many funerary inscriptions read "To speak the name of the dead is to make them live again," for it restores, "the breath of life to him who has vanished." Prayers inscribed on the outside of tombs often exhorted the passerby to speak the name of the man buried within. Sometimes where there was a political upheaval, the new ruler would try to obliterate the name of his hated predecessor by having the name cut out of all royal inscriptions. That was considered the ultimate punishment and revenge. It was a fate that King Tut suffered, and is one reason why so little was known about him.

By finding King Tut's tomb, Carter and Carnarvon made sure that the name of this obscure and otherwise unknown king would be remembered and spoken of throughout the entire world some 4,000 years after his death. Far from placing a curse on them, he should have granted them three wishes.

The legend of the mummy's curse, as it developed after the discovery of King Tut's tomb, has nothing about walking mummies. The belief, or fear, that the mummy was somehow going to get up, walk, and presumably physically strangle anyone who violated its tomb or otherwise displeased it is a comparatively modern one. There is absolutely nothing about walking mummies in ancient Egyptian literature or religion. Still it's not hard to see how and why the belief arose. Just walking through a museum exhibit of Egyptian mummies always provokes a shudder. Sure, you know they're all dead and have been for thousands of years. But you can't entirely suppress the thought that you will see a bandaged hand slowly push up the lid of a coffin, and suddenly the thing inside will sit up with a jerk and send you screaming in terror out of the Hall of Mummies.

The notion is an absurd one, of course, even though the ancient Egyptians went to extraordinary lengths to preserve the bodies of the dead in a lifelike fashion. A mummy is a poor candidate for reanimation. All the internal organs were removed from the corpse. A mummy is quite literally nothing but a hollow shell. The mummy was then stuffed, thoroughly dried, and wrapped in hundreds of yards of linen. After that, the mummy was placed in anywhere from one to half a dozen coffins, depending upon the wealth and importance of the dead person. For someone really important, like a king, the outer sarcophagus might be carved from solid rock and capped with a lid that weighed many tons. All of these mummy cases, as well as the tomb itself, were then carefully and hopefully permanently sealed. Even Count Dracula would have trouble getting out of a tomb like that.

Finally, there is the wrapping itself. The mummies were wrapped in a bundle, that is, the legs were wrapped together and the folded arms wrapped securely across the chest. In order to move at all, the mummy would first have to unwrap itself!

While the Egyptians went to great lengths to preserve the dead, the famous mummification process was really not as good as popular legend would lead one to believe. It was a fairly hit or miss affair. Sometimes it worked very well. An Egyptologist gazing on the remarkably well-preserved remains of the pharaoh Seti I, said, "I aver that many persons now living look more decayed."

On the other hand, King Tutankhamen's mummy was a mess. The ancient embalmers had poured on too many oils and resins, and rather than preserving the remains, they had hastened the decay. Parts of the mummy literally fell to dust at the touch.

From the early nineteenth century, when stories of

mummies and then the mummies themselves began appearing in Europe, they became objects of wonder and terror and sometimes entertainment. One English invitation, decorated with a picture of a mummy read: "Lord Londesborough, At Home, Monday, 10th June, 1850, 144 Piccadilly. A Mummy from Thebes to be unrolled at half past two."

There were tales of mummies come to life in Victorian-era thrill fiction. But what really fixed the image of the walking mummy, the resurrected corpse, was the movies and, in particular, one movie.

It was the film called, appropriately enough, *The Mummy*. It was made by Hollywood's Universal Pictures in 1932, and starred Boris Karloff, straight from his triumph as the monster in *Frankenstein*.

Actually, Karloff appears as a mummy, that is, a wrapped corpse, in only one brief scene—but that scene is a horror classic. The mummy of an ancient Egyptian priest called Imhotep has just been excavated, and it is being guarded at night by a young archaeologist. The young man is innocently reading aloud from a book of ancient spells, and quite accidentally he reads a spell for reviving the dead. Suddenly the eyes of the partially wrapped mummy open—Imhotep has come back to life.

Just exactly what happens next is never shown. All we see are the feet of the mummy, trailing torn wrappings, disappear through a door. The young archaeologist is so horrified by what he has experienced that he is reduced to giggling madness, saying things like, "He got up and took a walk."

For most of the film, Karloff is a completely unwrapped mummy, a tall, wizened, heavily wrinkled man, wearing a one-piece hanging garment and a fez on his head. But it is the reawakening scene and the dragging wrappings that everyone who has seen the film remembers.

The plot concerns the efforts of Imhotep to revive the mummy of his ancient love, Princess Ananka. Unfortunately, Ananka's spirit has taken possession of the body of Helen Grosvenor, the daughter of a prominent archaeologist. She must be killed first, before the ancient princess can be brought back to life. Love among the long dead, it seems, can become pretty complicated. It's not the plot of the film that counts. It's the way it looks.

The mummy makeup was created by Jack Pierce, who also created the classic makeup for the films *Frankenstein*, *The Wolf Man*, and many of the other Universal Pictures horror films of the 1930s and '40s It is these films that really set the style for all the films and television that was to follow. If you get nightmares about being chased by a mummy, blame Jack Pierce.

Pierce actually based his makeup on the appearance of a real mummy, that of Tuthmosis III. "The film is truer to the lore of ancient Egypt in its props than in its plot," complains Egyptologist Christine El Mahdy. "The Egyptians believed in an afterlife but not in the physical resurrection of mummies . . . Nevertheless, the film was probably the first introduction for a popular mass audience to the myth and magic of mummies."

At the end of the film the resurrected Imhotep is reduced to a pile of ashes by the goddess Isis. But as every fan of horror films knows, if a monster is popular he will somehow come back for the next film, no matter how thoroughly he was destroyed in the last film.

Karloff's *Mummy* was popular, and as you would expect, the Mummy returned for a whole cycle of films. But it was a series that went sharply downhill almost immediately. These films are more likely to provoke laughs than screams today, but at the time, they were considered quite frightening. The biggest loss in the later films was Karloff himself. He never played the Mummy again; that part was taken by Lon Chaney, Jr., who is best known for playing the anguished werewolf in the Wolf Man films. But the Mummy role took no acting skill at all.

In these films, the Mummy's name has been changed to Kharis, and he is nothing more than a grunting, bandaged, and hard to kill horror, who slowly, clumsily, but relentlessly stalks his victims over a variety of landscapes, including Connecticut. There was something oddly effective about the sight of an animated Egyptian mummy dragging its dirty wrappings past the clean white clapboard houses of Hollywood's version of Connecticut.

It is in the later films that the idea of the living mummy as the guardian of the tomb is established. Kharis is supposed to be guarding the tomb of Ananka. He kills one of the archaeologists who finds Ananka's tomb, but others are able to remove her mummy. When Ananka's mummy is taken to a museum in Connecticut, Kharis, with the help of the high priest of Amon-Ra, follows. It is the mummy's duty to punish all those who have violated her tomb. Now it is the mummy itself that has become the curse, or at least the agent that carries out the curse.

Kharis is kept alive by a solution made from the mystic tana leaves. These leaves are prepared on the night of the full moon with a ceremony that calls upon the name of Amon-Ra, and all the lesser gods of Egypt. The leaves are boiled over a slow fire in an ancient vessel made expressly for the ceremony. The solution that results is fed to the mummy. The fluid from three leaves will keep Kharis alive, while nine will give him movement and tremendous strength.

Despite the rather poor quality of the later mummy films, they were also extremely popular. In the 1950s, when Britain's Hammer Studios made its series of color remakes of all the classic black-and-white Universal monster films, *The Mummy* was among them. This time it was a well-wrapped Christopher Lee stalking not Egypt or Connecticut, but Britain.

As a monster, the Mummy was never as popular as the Frankenstein monster, Dracula, or the Wolf Man. But it does stand in the front rank of the second tier of movie monsters. And the films certainly fixed in all of our minds the image of what a mummy is supposed to look and act like.

And on rare occasions, a real mummy acts like we all think it is supposed to—it actually moves. One of those rare events took place in 1881. Archaeologists had uncovered an enormous cache of royal mummies that thousands of years ago had been hidden in a common tomb after their original tombs had been plundered by robbers. There were so many important mummies that the excavators didn't know what to do with them. Sometimes the mummies were just laid outside in the sand until caskets could be found.

The mummy of Ramses I lay in the sun so long that the wrappings and the resins began to heat up, and the mummy's arm slowly rose of its own accord. As you might imagine, that created quite a panic among the workmen.

But according to Egyptologist John A. Wilson, the best moving mummy story comes, not from Egypt but from Chicago.

"The macabre appearance of a mummy," he wrote, "excites the imagination of the superstitious, and there are stories about a mummy making a gesture or moving around at night. The only mummy that I ever heard of that did move was Peruvian not Egyptian. The story goes that the Field Museum [in Chicago] many years ago received a shipment of mummies from Peru. They had been crammed down into barrels, tightly flexed inside the wooden containers. The foreman of the basement workers said, 'Jim, knock the head off of one of those barrels. Let's see what's in them.' Jim went to work and loosened the head of a barrel. He had just succeeded in getting it free all the way around, when the head of the barrel flew off, a mummy rose up before him, making a whooshing noise as the air rushed into its body. With the release of the pressure, the body resumed its outstretched position. Jim left suddenly without discovering what the shipment was."

While it is Egyptian mummies that have always been regarded with dread, the mummies of Peru have not excited our imagination to the same degree. A lot of people don't even know that Peru has mummies. Yet between the two, it is the mummies of Peru that would seem to be the most likely candidates to get up and start walking around.

In Egypt, the mummies were either buried, or in the case of the high born, hidden away in elaborately constructed tombs. In Peru, the royal mummies were part of everyday life.

The Incas who ruled Peru before the coming of the Spanish had a curious belief about their dead kings. The kings were considered to be gods while they were alive, and as gods they could never really die. Someday, the Incas believed, all the dead kings would return. In the meantime, the king's mummy continued to possess a life of sorts.

Much of Inca society was organized around this belief. While the dead king's royal power passed to his legitimate heir, usually his oldest son, his wealth did not. The new ruler had only the wealth he had accumulated as prince. The bulk of the royal treasure and estates remained in the hands of his dead father and of the dead man's household that was to take care of the remains. As a result, dead kings were usually richer than living ones. The household of a dead king might number in the thousands. Just what might have happened to Inca society over the long run is impossible to know. It would seem that a great accumulation of vast wealth in the mummified hands of dead kings would have created serious problems. But because of the sudden arrival of the Spanish conquerors, the Inca empire didn't last very long. When it fell, there were only nine dead kings that had to be supported.

Before the conquest, the Inca king's mummy was

set up in one of his villas and was treated as a living being. An attendant in a golden mask always stood nearby to brush away any annoying flies from the mummy. It was served regular meals, and members of the household often asked it questions. The mummy replied to the questions through a specially appointed oracle, of course. During public ceremonies, the mummies of the kings were carried through the streets and spoke to the assembled crowds. Once again, it was the oracles who did the talking. But if one of these Peruvian mummies actually got up and started walking around, people probably wouldn't have been too surprised.

3
▼ ▼
The Zombie

"Hold that man. Don't let him go,
heavenly judge, hold that man."

The zombie (or zombi) is the ultimate walking
corpse. Unlike the Frankenstein monster and
the walking mummy, the zombie is not a creation of fiction, fantasy, or films. Belief in the zombie
grew out of voodoo, a complex collection of religious
and magical practices that have flourished on the island nation of Haiti, and to a lesser extent in the city
of New Orleans.

Voodoo is shot through with visions of death and
the cemetery. This should not be surprising, coming
as it does from a land which has such a tragic and
brutal history. The voodoo god of death is Baron Samedi. His *veve*—the ceremonial emblem containing
his symbols, the skull and crossbones—can be found

in most graveyards in Haiti. The Baron himself is often depicted as a tall man dressed as an undertaker, with a black frock coat, bowler hat, and carrying a walking stick.

In addition to being lord of the cemetery, Baron Samedi is the deity that controls zombies. Both the word *zombie* and the word *samedi* come from the same Indian word *zemi*, which connotes both the spirit of the dead and the familiar soulless "walking dead."

The voodoo religion is a rich and constantly evolving set of beliefs drawn from many sources. The basic inspiration for voodoo is the religious beliefs that African slaves brought with them when they were transported to the New World. To the basic African religion (or more accurately, religions, for the slaves had come from different parts of Africa and held different beliefs) was added the religion to which their masters forcibly converted them. In Haiti, that was Catholicism as practiced in France.

Still another influence on modern voodoo is eighteenth-, nineteenth-, and even twentieth-century occultism, for voodoo is always absorbing new influences. The British anthropologist Francis Huxley, who studied voodoo in Haiti in the 1970s, wrote in his book *The Invisibles, The Voodoo Gods of Haiti*, "French books on occultism creep into Haiti every year, with their load of fusty names and dark secrets;

there are books on palmistry, yoga, divination by tea leaves or coffee grounds . . ."

Therefore, it is difficult to make many broad pronouncements about voodoo, since it does not have set doctrines, articles of faith, or regular priesthood. Voodoo has also been the subject of sensationalism, exploitation, and misunderstanding, much of it deliberate. Indeed, the whole idea of the zombie is not really a basic part of the voodoo religion at all. But there are some voodoo beliefs which lend plausibility to the belief that a corpse can be reanimated and given a semblance of life.

The voodoo religion has a very complicated view of life after death. The soul does not go to some remote place where it receives its reward or punishment; indeed, the soul is not a single entity at all. A part of what we call the soul may continue to reside with the family of the dead and must be honored with various sacrifices and rituals. This is really a form of ancestor worship common in Africa and elsewhere in the world.

Not all ancestors are honored equally, and after a few years undistinguished ones are forgotten entirely, while more celebrated ancestors may be turned into gods worshipped even by those outside of the immediate family. Baron Samedi himself may have been a real person, perhaps a powerful voodoo priest, or *houngan*. Many of the gods of voodoo appear to have begun this way.

While the Haitian voodooist is more comfortable with the spirits of the dead than those raised in the Judeo/Christian tradition are with the thought of ghosts, the dead body or *corps cadavre* is quite another matter. Deprived of its soul, the body is like a car without a driver; it can be stolen and used by a new owner. This is particularly true in the first few days after death, before the body has begun to seriously decompose. The new owner gains possession of the body by magic, and that is where voodoo comes in. Beliefs about the bodies of the newly dead being vulnerable to some sort of possession were common throughout Europe several hundred years ago, but today, if such beliefs survive at all, they are limited to remote regions. In Haiti, the belief is very much alive.

Magic plays a significant role in voodoo. The houngan not only conducts ceremonies in which the celebrants are put in contact with the gods, he or she is also credited with possessing a great deal of magical knowledge. The houngan brews substances to cure disease and make charms, to defeat enemies, or to attract lovers. And some houngans are supposed to have the power to make corpses into zombies.

To those of us who were brought up on Hollywood horror films, the zombie is a figure of supernatural evil, a monster that stands alongside the Frankenstein monster, Count Dracula, the Wolf Man, and the mummy. But unlike most supernatural monsters, the zombie is not inherently evil; he is a flesh-and-blood robot, an automaton completely under the control of the voodoo priest, who can use him for good or evil.

To make a zombie, a fresh corpse is stolen from a graveyard, with the proper ceremonies. Those digging up the grave chant to Baron Samedi, asking him to "hold that man. Don't let him go, heavenly judge, hold that man." It is a plea to the lord of the cemetery to let the corpse retain that part of its spirit that will allow it to be reanimated as a zombie.

The corpse is taken to the home of the houngan, and through the use of secret spells, incantations, and perhaps magical drugs, the corpse can be made to move, to take on a semblance of life. Zombies are often called "the living dead," but this is a misnomer. According to Haitian folklore, their zombie is not truly alive; it is merely a corpse that can be made to move at the command of its master. The zombie is mindless, soulless, and heartless.

Tradition holds that zombies were first created for working in the sugarcane fields. They needed neither rest nor food; they were tireless and supernaturally strong. But making use of zombies was illegal, so it was believed that they were used in the fields only at night when they would not attract the attention of the authorities. Bakers were often rumored to use zombie labor, since a baker does most of his work at night and the bake oven fires can be seen flickering in the darkness.

Despite the zombie's reputation for being mindless, there are stories of zombies being used as bookkeepers, and there is a fairly recent report of a zombie being found working in a clothes shop.

The zombie is also supposed to regain his power of speech after he tastes salt. Salt is considered a powerful magic substance in many cultures. There is one tale of an overseer of zombie laborers who accidentally gave them salt. They regained not only their power of speech, but an awareness of what they were. They made their way back to the graves from which they were stolen, and tried to dig their way under the ground until their fingers rotted. In the morning the half-rotted corpses were found sprawled over the graves.

In much zombie lore the zombies are treated as slaves. They are beaten regularly in order to assure their obedience.

The origin of the zombie legend is unclear, for there seems to be nothing quite like it in either African or European folklore. Says Huxley of zombies ". . . they are slaves, and the folklore surrounding them is partly a reminiscence of plantation days when the Negroes learnt to endure forced labour, punishments and the whimsical cruelties by acting stupid and not allowing their resentment to show itself. Nowadays what better slaves can there be than the dead, if you know how to constrain them?"

In Huxley's view, the zombie is a horrific caricature

of a slave as he was often forced to behave in order to survive. The zombie also seems to be a slave's worst nightmare. For the slave, the only hope of release from a grinding and cruel existence was death and the promise of a blissful afterlife. But if a dead slave's body was reanimated for labor after death as a zombie, than the slave existence would continue, perhaps for all eternity. It is a particularly ghastly and frightening vision.

It has also been speculated that the zombie tales were used by slaves to frighten their masters, and by voodoo priests to scare restless followers into submission. The houngan might threaten to send a zombie after his enemies or to turn them into zombies after they died.

Then there are the more sensational theories that the legend of the zombie is not a legend at all, but based on things that really happened, and perhaps are still happening. In 1985, Wade Davis, a young Harvard-educated anthropologist, said that he had discovered the zombie drug—the substance used by the voodoo priests to turn people into zombies—and that he had penetrated the secrets of how and why zombies were created.

Davis decided to go on his quest for the secret of the zombies after being shown several accounts of apparently authentic Haitian zombies in recent times. The first was the case of a man named Clairvius Narcisse who, according to a death certificate, died in 1962. The problem was that twenty years later Narcisse was alive and resettled with his family. Both he and his family claimed that he was the victim of a voodoo cult, and that immediately following his burial he was taken from the grave as a zombie.

In the spring of 1962, Narcisse, then aged about forty, went to the emergency entrance of the Albert Schweitzer Hospital near his home. He was complaining of fever and body aches and he had begun to spit blood. His condition deteriorated rapidly and on May 2 he was pronounced dead by two attendant physicians. His older sister, Angelina Narcisse, witnessed the body and approved the official death certificate. The body was placed in cold storage and buried twenty-four hours later in a small local cemetery.

In 1980, eighteen years later, a man walked into the market-place and approached Angelina Narcisse. He said that he was her supposedly dead brother, and he was able to supply details about the family that only a family member would have known. He said that he had been made into a zombie at the orders of his older brother, with whom he had been having a land dispute. The "zombification" had been carried out by members of a secret, but powerful, voodoo cult. First, they had poisoned him with the zombie drug. Then they took him from his grave, beat and bound him, and then led him away to the north of the country where he worked as a slave for two years with other zombies. Eventually, the zombie master was killed and the zombies were freed from whatever force bound them. Narcisse spent the next sixteen years wandering about the country. It was only when he heard that his older brother died that he dared go back to his native village. The case generated a good deal of publicity in Haiti, and was the subject of a BBC documentary in 1981.

The Narcisse case was the most well-documented, but Davis was shown other recent zombie cases as well. A woman named Natagette Joseph, who was supposed to have been killed as the result of a land dispute in 1966, was found wandering around her home village in 1980 by the police officer who, fourteen years earlier, had pronounced her dead.

A woman known by the nickname "Ti Femme" was pronounced dead at age thirty on February 23, 1976. Her mother found her three years later, recognizing her by a childhood scar on her temple. When her grave was opened, her coffin was found to be full of rocks.

In 1980, Haitian radio reported the discovery of a strange group of individuals who were wandering aimlessly near the north coast of the country. The local peasants identified them as zombies. They were placed under the charge of the army, and after an extensive publicity campaign, most of the reputed zombies were identified and returned to their home villages, many of the villages a long distance from where the zombies had been found.

There are many possible "rational" explanations for all of these stories. After extensive research in Haiti, Davis believed that he was able to identify the "zombie drug," a substance that could put people in a deathlike state. Davis believed that a combination of the drug and the brutal treatment they received after they were "revived" could destroy people's minds and reduce them to a zombielike state.

The drug and the magical ceremonies that accompanied the zombie ritual were controlled by the secretive but powerful cult. In Davis's view, the zombie was not really a kind of cheap labor. In poverty-stricken Haiti, cheap labor abounds. The cult uses the fear of being made a zombie as a threat to terrify and control those who would oppose them. Becoming a zombie is quite literally the "fate worse than death."

The "real" zombie stories which had inspired Davis to go to Haiti and investigate the phenomena are not the only, or even the most famous, accounts of this type. Probably the most notorious of all the "real" zombie accounts concerns a young woman known only as Marie M., the daughter of a prominent Haitian family, who died in 1909. Five years after her death, a former schoolmate of Marie's reported seeing her in a house in Port-au-Prince, the capital city of Haiti. There was a great public outcry and the house was searched. The owner had fled and the house was empty.

Marie's grave was opened and a skeleton was found in the coffin, but people said that it was not the skeleton of the girl, for it was too large for the box in which it had been buried. Also, the clothes in which Marie had been buried were found neatly folded up and laid alongside the skeleton. Many people believed that another body had been placed in the grave to cover up the crime of stealing Marie's body.

The rumors continued. It was reported that Marie had been turned into a zombie by a famous houngan who had since died. The houngan's wife had no use for the zombies her husband had created. She went to a Catholic priest for advice. The priest told her that the zombies had to be freed from their unnatural state. But how was this to be accomplished? It was while the priest was pondering the problem that Marie was first sighted. When the public scandal erupted, the zombie that had once been Marie M. was disguised in the habit of a nun and smuggled secretly out of the country to France. Later, her brother claimed that he had seen her in a French convent. Like so many zombie stories, however, there is little solid evidence to support it. We don't even know the full name of the girl who was supposed to have been made into a zombie.

Another celebrated zombie case was related by the African-American writer Zora Neale Hurston in her book about Haiti, *Tell My Horse*. This case concerns a young woman named Felicia Felix-Mentor, who died in 1907. Twenty-nine years later, a woman turned up on the farm owned by the dead woman's family and said, "This is the farm of my father. I used to live here."

At first, workmen on the farm tried to drive the strange woman away. But then the owner arrived and he recognized the woman as his long-dead sister. Doctors were sent for and the woman was taken to a hospital. Finally, her husband confirmed the identification, though he was reluctant to do so. He was immediately suspected of being an accomplice in the crime of turning his wife into a zombie, though nothing could be proved.

When she heard the story, Miss Hurston decided to visit the hospital where the zombie was being kept.

"We found the Zombie in the hospital yard. They had just set her dinner before her but she was not eating. She hovered against the fence in a sort of defensive position . . . The doctor uncovered her head for a moment but she promptly clapped her arms over it to shut out the things she dreaded . . . Finally the doctor forcibly uncovered her so that I could [take a picture] of her face, and the sight was dreadful. That blank face with its dead eyes. The eyelids were white all around the eyes as if they had been burned with acid."

The doctors at the institution did not really think that the woman was an example of the living dead. They believed that she had been given some sort of drug that simulated death, and that she was later "revived." One doctor described the drug as "some secret probably brought from Africa and handed down from generation to generation. These men know the effect of the drug and its antidote. It is evident that it destroys that part of the brain which governs speech and willpower. The victims can move and act but cannot formulate thought." Many years later, Wade Davis came to pretty much the same conclusion.

Davis first went to Haiti to try and provide the sort of solid evidence that other investigators of the zombie phenomena had been unable to find. But Davis failed in what had been his original objective, and in what would have provided the conclusive proof of his theory. "I failed to document a zombi as it was taken from the cemetery."

He said that he had been offered two opportunities to view the process, but it would have cost a lot of money. What if he was shown a fake? There is a long history of fake zombie ceremonies being staged for gullible and sensation-seeking tourists in Haiti. Then he would have wasted his money. On the other hand, if it was real "I would have no way of being certain that the money had not been responsible for the victim's fate." That was an ethical barrier Davis felt that he was unable to cross.

When he visited Haiti, Huxley too was told that he would be shown a zombie, but at a very high price. One houngan finally offered to show him a zombie at a reasonable price, but when Huxley said that he wanted to photograph the zombie, the houngan simply walked away.

Huxley's sophisticated Haitian friends didn't believe in zombies at all, and said that such tales were concocted to frighten children.

"If someone says he can show you a zombie, Sal [one of Huxley's Haitian friends] went on, it is a *combinaison* [conspiracy]. It'll be in the cemetery and after you've been led around the graves, a man in a white sheet will come out and go Hoo."

In one of the towns, Huxley talked to a magistrate who said that he had once seen the corpse of a man supposedly enchanted or poisoned to death, then dug up and successfully reanimated. But the next morning, when he examined the grave, he found a pipe leading from the coffin to the air, so that the "corpse" could breathe while buried. Frauds like this must have inspired many of the horror tales that have come out of Haiti over the years.

While the zombie of Haiti is certainly the most famous of all the walking dead beliefs, animated corpses of one sort or another figure in the lore of many nations. There are, for example, the "walkers after death" of northern European folklore. These beings are not really ghosts, though they are supposed to possess many powers that are considered supernatural. They are the animated corpses of evil people who have frozen to death in the bitter cold of the northern winter. They haunt, or more accurately, stalk isolated farms and cabins, and try to drag the living from the warmth of their firesides into the outside cold, which is the realm of the "walkers after death."

Animated corpses are thoroughly mixed into European vampire lore. Those of us who grew up on Dracula films think of the vampire as an elegant, even romantic, figure. But in much of Central Europe, where people really believed in vampires, the creature was a stinking, shambling, half-rotted corpse that had just dug its way out of the grave, and not only drained blood but spread disease wherever it went.

In China, any unburied corpse was in danger of being possessed by evil spirits and being turned into a monstrous creature called a *Ch'iang Shich*. These creatures had greenish skin, glowing eyes, and a breath so foul that it caused instant death.

Zombies appeared in a number of horror films. Some of them, like *White Zombie* (1932) and *I Walked with a Zombie* (1943), are really quite good. But the zombie never really made the first rank of movie monsters. However, the film zombie was given a whole new lease on afterlife in 1968 with an independently produced low-budget film called *Night of the Living Dead*, directed by George Romero. This film, which featured hordes of flesh-eating zombies roaming the countryside, became a cult classic, and spawned hordes of sequels and imitators. It is one of the touchstone modern horror films. Considered shockingly gruesome in its time, it seems fairly mild by today's standards, but it is still not a film to be watched at night alone.

4

▼ ▼

The Artificial Man

"This is one of the great secrets, and it ought
to remain a secret until the days approach when
all secrets will be known."

The underlying theme of Mary Shelley's *Frankenstein*, and indeed of all tales of mad scientists or evil magicians and their creations, is that they have somehow "gone too far." In creating or attempting to create life or a semblance of life, they have obtained "forbidden knowledge" and have trespassed on the realm of God or the gods. And, usually, they have been horribly punished for their arrogance.

One of the oldest explorations of this theme is in the ancient Greek myth of Prometheus. Prometheus was the god who revolted against Zeus, the chief god, and stole the fire from heaven. Zeus devised a particularly ghastly retribution. He had Prometheus chained to a mountaintop in the Caucasus. Every day he would be attacked by a vulture which would devour his liver piece by piece. Every night his liver grew back, so that the punishment could be prolonged for eternity. Zeus was not a god known for his mercy.

In the Roman version of the same myth, Prometheus created or recreated mankind by animating a figure of clay. By about the third century A.D., the two elements of the legend had been fused together; the fire stolen by Prometheus became the fire of life.

Mary Shelley certainly knew about the myth and its implications, and subtitled her famous novel *The Modern Prometheus.*

A version of the clay figure brought to life also found its way into the medieval Jewish legends of the golem. The golem is a gigantic and brutish figure, more like the mute monster of the Frankenstein films than the gabby complainer of the novel. According to the tradition, various holy men were able to animate a figure made from clay through the use of the secret and sacred name of God.

The idea of the golem was clearly inspired by the description in the *Book of Genesis* where God creates Adam by making a figure from the "dust of the ground" and then breathing life into his nostrils. But a creature, created in this way by humans, could not be fully human—for that would imply that humans could possess Godlike powers. The golem, while animate, was much less than human, sometimes dangerously so.

As the tales became more elaborate, certain rabbis were credited with being able to control the life-giving force. They would first dance around the figure, pronouncing holy words. Finally, they would bring the creature to life by writing the Hebrew word "Emeth," which means truth, on its forehead. The creature then became the loyal servant of his master.

The golem of legend is a rather zombielike creature, without the power of speech or any will of its own. And unlike Frankenstein's creation, it was quite easy to get rid of. All the rabbi had to do was erase the "E" from its forehead. Without the letter "E" the inscription read "meth" which means death. The monster would immediately be deprived of life and turn back into a clay figure, which would fall to the ground.

Despite the ease with which the creature could be destroyed, one of the most famous of the golem tales has it turning, Frankenstein-like, on its creator. In the story *The Golem of Chelm*, set in the sixteenth century, Rabbi Elijah writes the secret word on a piece of parchment, which he places on the monster's forehead. This golem, however, is no docile servant. It is a true monster and wreaks havoc on the city of Chelm, and on the rabbi who made it. In one version of the tale, the rabbi is killed by a blow from the out-of-control golem. In another version the rabbi tries to destroy the giant by a trick. He orders it to take off its boots and while the monster is bending over, he manages to wipe the letter "E" from the inscription on the parchment. The monster immediately collapses to the ground, crushing the unfortunate rabbi.

But by far the most famous of all the golem stories is that of the monster brought to life by Rabbi Low of Prague. Rabbi Low was a real historical figure who died in 1609. In the story of the golem of Prague, Rabbi Low created the creature to protect his people from those who would harm them. At the time, the Jews were suffering terrible persecution. The golem was to prowl the streets of the Jewish ghetto, warding off possible attackers.

The ceremony by which the clay figure was brought to life has been described in some detail. First, the rabbi has leading figures in the community walk around the figure reciting sacred charms.

"Then Rabbi Low himself walked once around the figure, placed in its mouth a piece of parchment inscribed with the *Schem* (the name of God); and bowing to the East and the West, the South and the North, recited, 'And he breathed into his nostrils the breath of life, and man became a living soul.'"

According to the legend, the golem could not be used by the rabbi for nonsacred tasks. But then, as in all of these stories, no matter what culture or period of time they come from, something goes horribly wrong. In this case, the golem rages out of control and threatens to demolish the entire Jewish quarter of the city. Rabbi Low hears of the disaster while he is in the middle of a service at the synagogue. He rushes out to destroy the monster by removing the parchment with the sacred word from its mouth. Once this task is completed, the pious rabbi rushes back to the synagogue to finish the interrupted service.

The tale of Rabbi Low and the golem of Prague has been the basis for many novels, plays, and even a few films. And the legend seems to have gained an extraordinary hold in the city of Prague itself.

In 1968, the press reported that a respectable engineer who lived on the famed Alchemists Street in Prague was crushed under the debris of a red clay statue. A police investigator told journalists that he saw the statue melt into a reddish shapeless mass of dust. Neighbors on the street talked of "the return of the golem," which is supposed to appear and walk the street whenever some major event is about to disrupt the city. There was an uprising in Prague in 1968.

More recently, an investigator said that while exploring the old synagogue that had been associated with Rabbi Low, he had discovered a small, prison-like, secret room at the top of the building. The room had previously been unknown, or at least unreported, and he theorized that someone—or something—had once been kept there.

In the 1935 film *The Bride of Frankenstein*, Dr. Pretorious, that maddest of all the screen's mad scientists, shows Frankenstein a collection of tiny humans that he has created. He keeps them in bottles, and "the king," a doll-sized replica of King Henry VIII, keeps trying to get out of his bottle and into the bottle containing one of the female figures. These tiny things, Pretorious ruefully admits, are nothing when compared to the giant-sized creature created by Frankenstein. It's a comic scene in the film, and in some ways a puzzling one. At least it seems puzzling until you realize that the creation of small human beings—the *homunculus* or "little man"—was something that really had been attempted, and, if all the stories are to be believed—actually accomplished.

The alchemists, in addition to trying to make gold from lead and discover the Elixir of Life, also tried to create the homunculus. It seemed a perfectly reasonable possibility to them, but it was based, as were most other alchemical beliefs, on a completely erroneous theory of how nature works.

The alchemists believed that all life was animated by some sort of "vital spirit." They thought if this "spirit" could somehow be isolated, and nurtured properly, it could become a living being.

Theophrastus Bombastus von Hohenheim (1493–

1541), mercifully known to history as Paracelsus, is generally regarded as history's greatest alchemist. His writings fascinated generations of would-be alchemists and occultists, and in Mary Shelley's novel he was one of Victor Frankenstein's heroes.

Paracelsus had a very precise formula for creating a homunculus. The alchemist puts the vital spirit in a hermetically sealed glass container and buries it in horse manure for about forty days. Don't snicker now; Paracelsus was serious, he was not putting us on. The rotting manure generates warmth, which will keep the container at an even heat. "After such a time," he wrote "it bears the form and resemblance of a human being, but will be transparent and without corpus."

It is now artificially fed *arcanium sanguinis homiunis* (one of those mysterious alchemical "essences") until it is about forty weeks old, "and if allowed to remain during that time in the horse manure, in a continually even temperature, it will grow into a human child, with all the members developed like any other child, such as may have been born of woman, only it will be much smaller. We call such a being a homunculus, and he may be raised and educated like any other child, until he grows older and obtains reason and intellect, and is able to take care of himself. This is one of the great secrets, and it ought to remain a secret until the days approach when all secrets will be known."

Cornelius Agrippa (1486–1535) had more of a reputation as a magician than an alchemist, but he, too, had a formula for producing the homunculus. Agrippa suggested the use of a mandrake root. This root was long believed to have magical properties because sometimes it can be shaped like a human figure. According to Agrippa, the root had to be specially prepared. It had to be dug up on a Friday morning before dawn by a black dog. The root was then washed, fed with milk and honey (or in some versions with human blood), and it would slowly evolve into a being about the size of a human infant. It then had to be kept in a secret place, and it looked after the well-being of its owner. Fraudulent objects—usually a mandrake root dressed in doll clothes—were sometimes sold by magical charlatans.

By 1775, what is called the Age of Reason was in full flower in Europe. Practices like magic and alchemy had long been discredited by the educated. Yet that was the year in which the most notorious of all the homunculus cases was supposed to have taken place. In Austria, two latter-day alchemists, Count Johann Ferdinand von Kufstein and Abbé Geloni claimed to have produced at least ten homunculi in only five weeks.

The little creatures were grown in large fruit jars full of water. The count and the abbé gave identities to their little creations. They included a king, a queen, a knight, a monk, a nun, and so on.

At first, the homunculi were only about six inches tall, so Count von Kufstein decided to have them grow larger. He buried the jars under two cartloads of manure. The two alchemists treated the manure heap with a special fluid made from what was described as "very disgusting materials." When the jars were dug out, the homunculi had almost doubled in size, and the males had grown heavy beards.

Tiny clothing was made for the creatures, appropriate to their roles—the king had king's robes, etc. They were fed every three or four days on some pink tablets that had been specially made for them. Every week the water in the jars was changed. It is not clear whether their clothes were waterproof.

The Austrian homunculi were able to reveal knowledge to their masters. They were specialists—the king talked only about politics, the knight about war, the monk about religion, and so on. But they possessed human desires. The king made several attempts to break out of his jar and into the jar of the queen. One day Count von Kufstein's butler, Joseph Kammerer, found the king out of his bottle clawing at the seal of the queen's container. The count and his servant chased the tiny monarch around the room, but were only able to catch him when the homunculus fainted, due to prolonged exposure with the air.

Now about this time you are doubtless beginning to figure that we have left the realm not only of reality but of genuine legend, and have entered the world of pure fantasy. And you're probably right. But there are documents indicating that there were those who took the story very seriously, and there are signed testimonials from some distinguished individuals insisting that they actually saw the ten homunculi.

This eighteenth-century story certainly inspired the scene in *Bride of Frankenstein* where Dr. Pretorious shows his young colleague, Dr. Frankenstein, his collection of little men and women in jars.

5

▼ ▼

The Sleeping Hero

"Mystery to the world, a grave for Arthur"

At one time it was quite common for a people who had lost or were losing a war to say, and perhaps to believe, that their heroes of the past were not really dead, but only sleeping, and would return at some time in the future when they were needed most. The myth of the sleeping hero can be an exceptionally powerful one.

Of all the sleeping hero legends, none is more persistent, more haunting, or more mysterious than that which surrounds King Arthur. But before we can decide whether King Arthur is really dead, or just asleep, we must tackle the question of whether King Arthur ever lived in the first place.

When you think of King Arthur and his Knights of

the Round Table, the image that springs to mind is a bunch of guys clanking around in medieval armor. That Arthur never existed. The medieval period in England, the fourteenth and fifteenth centuries, is quite well-documented. There is absolutely no authentic record of a King Arthur in England or of a Round Table or a place called Camelot during that period.

The legends about King Arthur are much older. It's just that the most complete and popular of the King Arthur legends were set in that period, and that is the picture that has been fixed in our minds ever since.

For generations, scholars have been searching for a "real" King Arthur, a historical figure who was the spark for all the later legends. The search has been a difficult one, in part because Arthur has been such a popular character that there were countless stories about him. For hundreds of years the British, the French, the Italians, and practically everyone else in Europe added something to the tales surrounding the legendary king's life and death. The result has been an incredibly tangled mass of legends, myths, folklore, local boosterism, hoax, and, here and there, a little bit of authentic history.

Most of the scholars who have studied the subject now believe that the stories of King Arthur can ultimately be traced back to the sixth century—the darkest of the Dark Ages—a period when civilization and Christianity throughout the old Roman Empire was crumbling in the face of barbarian invaders. Records of any kind from this era are fragmentary and unreliable, but they do contain hints about the life and career of the "real" Arthur.

The historical Arthur was not a great king ruling a unified Britain. It is far more likely that he was a minor, though relatively successful, leader of the Romanized and Christian Britons in their war against the pagan Saxon invaders, sometime during the sixth century.

Arthur may well have been the best war leader the Britons had at that time and, according to later accounts, he won some important battles. But the cause he was fighting for was a lost one. He was killed, and ultimately the Saxons overwhelmed the Britons, became Christians themselves, and were in turn conquered by the Norman invaders a few hundred years later.

At the time of Arthur's death, the Britons were hard-pressed, and the loss of a leader of Arthur's stature would have been a painful blow. The records seem to indicate that Arthur was not killed in a battle with the invaders, but rather in a fight with members of his own family, not an uncommon fate for leaders of that era. It is not unreasonable to suppose that Arthur's followers tried to hide the loss from their opponents, and even from many of their own supporters, to keep them from becoming discouraged.

It was common for victors to display the bodies, or in some cases just the heads, of slain or executed enemies, not just to terrorize the population—though that certainly would have been one result—but to prove that the person really was dead. If there was no body, how could one be sure? Perhaps the person really wasn't dead; perhaps he was just wounded or hiding and would return.

In any event, very early on, the tradition developed that Arthur had not really died, that he had only been wounded, and taken off somewhere safe to recover and fight again another day. However, the belief that the wounded hero will be healed and come back begins to wear thin after a few hundred years. So a supernatural element inevitably enters the story. The king is not dead, only sleeping. As long as no one could prove that Arthur's body actually lay beneath the ground, the fiction that he might still be alive in some way could be maintained. Keeping Arthur's burial site a secret, therefore, would have been an extremely important political act. An old poem called "The Song of Graves" contains this line, "A mystery to the world, a grave for Arthur."

A monk called Geoffrey of Monmouth was the first to compile an extensive chronicle of Arthur's deeds, though Geoffrey himself lived a full six hundred years after Arthur's time and had to depend entirely on sources that are now lost to us. We have no idea how accurate his account is.

Geoffrey had this to say about the hero's final appearance in history. After a furious battle:

"Even the renowned King Arthur himself was wounded deadly and was borne thence unto the island of Avalon for the healing of his wounds, where he gave up the crown unto his kinsman, Constantine, son of Cador, in A.D. 542."

Over the centuries this fairly simple scene became more and more elaborate, and more magical. In a much later version, the gravely wounded Arthur gives his famous sword, Excalibur, to Sir Bedevere and commands him to throw it into the water. When the faithful knight does as he is ordered, a hand appears out of the water and seizes Excalibur in the air. Without a ripple both hand and sword vanish.

Bedevere then carries the King to the edge of the water and they both watch as a silk-draped boat glides out of the mist. In the boat are tall women cloaked in black. They take the wounded king in their arms, carry him to the boat, and disappear over the waters.

Bedevere thought—and others thought—the King had not died. The women were the company of the enchantress Morgan le Fey, who took Arthur to the Isle of Avalon, the Island of Apples, to heal and protect him until England needed him again. Morgan le Fey appears as an evil enchantress and enemy of Arthur in many tales, but in this version she is good.

Obviously, we have now entered the realm of fantasy and fairy tale. But one thing is clear in all the tales. The Isle of Avalon is not some realm for the spirits of dead heroes, because Arthur is not dead. He is either "sleeping" or being kept alive by some sort of magic. Scholars have tried to uncover what kernels of truth may lie behind the myths. If Arthur was real, and he apparently was, where did he die? What happened to his body? And why was the belief that he had never died so persistent?

The Isle of Avalon has been "located" by many different writers. Several have said that it is really the Mediterranean island of Sicily, and a few travelers reported actually meeting Arthur there. It is more reasonable, however, to look for Avalon closer to Arthur's home of England.

The number one candidate is a place called Glastonbury. It is the site of a very ancient abbey, one of the earliest Christian sites in the British Isles. Before that, it had apparently been a major pagan sanctuary. It was common for Christian missionaries to plant their own establishments right on top of the temples or holy places of their pagan rivals. It was also common for ordinary folk to become confused about the traditions of rival religious systems, so pagan and Christian beliefs often were merged so thoroughly that it is no longer possible to separate them.

One immediate problem with the identification of

Glastonbury with the Isle of Avalon is that Glastonbury today isn't an island. But at one time Glastonbury tor, or hill, stuck out as the only dry spot in
miles of marshland (now drained). It could easily
have been considered an island in Arthur's time.

While Arthur and his followers were unquestion-
ably Christian, their Christianity may not have been
very deep. They may well have incorporated old ideas
about Glastonbury as some sort of mystic Isle of Avalon. If Arthur's fatal battle had been fought anywhere in the region known as Somersetshire, as is
quite likely, he would almost certainly have been
brought to Glastonbury for burial. It was the most
prominent religious house anywhere in the area, a
fitting place to bury a fallen chief. And if Arthur's
lieutenants wanted to hide news of the death of their
leader, the burial could have been conducted secretly.

There is another possible connection between the
idea of an undead Arthur with Glastonbury. Glastonbury has, for centuries, been associated with St. Joseph of Arimathea. He is the man who is supposed
to have given his tomb to Jesus' disciples as the place
for His body to be laid after the crucifixion. That was
the tomb that, three days later, was found empty.
This is one of the most important incidents in Christian history and is described in detail in all four
Gospels.

In early Christian Britain, the legend arose that St.

Joseph of Arimathea had come to the British Isles after the crucifixion, carrying with him the Holy Grail, which he deposited in Glastonbury. The Holy Grail legend was later to become an integral part of Arthurian lore. The association of this particular saint with Glastonbury may have served to remind early Christians in Britain of the significance of an empty tomb.

No one in a thoroughly Christianized England was going to claim that Arthur had risen from the dead. To have preached such a message would have been shockingly blasphemous, and in some eras it would have been an offense that could lead to being burned at the stake. But to say that Arthur was not really dead, but merely "sleeping"—that was different. Such a belief skirted the problem of blasphemy.

Historically, the monks of Glastonbury supported the idea that Arthur had been brought to their abbey—but that he was well and truly dead and had been buried there. The "tomb" of King Arthur has been discovered at Glastonbury, not once but several times.

The first time was around 1192. The monks were supposed to have discovered the graves of Arthur and his queen in the old Celtic burial ground within the confines of the abbey. The reigning monarch at the time, Richard I, ordered the abbot to have the remains removed to a more fitting tomb.

In the year 1278, King Edward I of England watched while the monks opened this new tomb and removed the remains of Arthur and his queen and placed them in the treasury of the abbey until an even more splendid resting place could be constructed.

The monk Adam of Domerham probably an eyewitness to the scene, left this description:

". . . the lord king had the tomb of the famous King Arthur opened. Wherein in two caskets painted with their pictures and arms, were found separately the bones of said king, which were of great size and those of Queen Guinevere, which were of marvelous beauty . . ."

It takes quite a stretch of the imagination to describe six-hundred-year-old bones as beautiful. It is doubtful if bones of any description could have survived intact from Arthur's time in the British climate. And, by the way, most scholars doubt if there ever was a Queen Guinevere at all. She is never mentioned until the Arthurian legend had been around for centuries.

Some years after the disinterment ordered by Edward I, the bones were placed in yet another tomb, which survived until the monastery was dissolved by King Henry VIII in 1536. At that time, the tomb was destroyed and any relics it contained were scattered. What is alleged to be the site of the tomb, however, now has an historical marker that visitors can see while viewing the impressive ruins of the ancient monastery itself. The marker is all that remains of King Arthur's grave and the final monument to this intriguing historical mystery.

The restless movement of what were supposed to be the remains of King Arthur from tomb to tomb may have been, in part, an attempt by later monarchs to honor and thus associate themselves with a glorious predecessor. It may also have been motivated by a desire for later kings to prove that Arthur's remains really were in the tomb, that he was dead and he wasn't coming back under any circumstances.

Though one can build an attractive case for the burial of King Arthur at Glastonbury, there are problems with such a theory as well. If Arthur had been buried at Glastonbury, then the monks would have known about it, even if others did not. Yet, for nearly six hundred years, though we have many documents from and about Glastonbury, there is no hint of the grave of King Arthur. Then in 1191, there was a disastrous fire at the abbey. Shortly thereafter, the monks announced that they had found the remains of Arthur and his queen. The "discovery" of this gravesite on the grounds of the abbey was bound to result in a good deal of favorable attention, as well as considerable funds to aid in rebuilding. The monks had a good reason for faking a find, and monkish forgeries are hardly unknown from that era.

There is another possible reason for faking a find. It is interesting to note that both times Arthur's alleged remains were removed, it was under the special direction of the reigning king. Why was the king so interested? Because the real Arthur had almost certainly been leader of the people who considered themselves Celts. The Celts lost to the Saxons, who in turn were subdued by the Normans. So the reigning kings of England were not Celts, but the Celtic people themselves, though defeated, had not disappeared. A measure of Celtic independence was maintained both in Scotland and Wales, outlying areas of Great Britain that for hundreds of years remained semi-independent of the English rulers, and often hostile to them. Scotland and Wales were potential sources of trouble for every reigning English monarch for centuries, and one can still find a great deal of Scottish and Welsh nationalism even today. The legends of the sleeping Arthur, who would someday return to lead his Celtic followers to victory against the hated English, flourished for centuries in Scotland and Wales. Such legends have always possessed a powerful revolutionary potential.

To finally and fully lay the bones of King Arthur to rest would have been a worthwhile accomplishment for any English monarch. One had to be careful and respectful, however, for in the twelfth and thirteenth centuries, Arthur was universally admired by the people of England. Besides, showing disrespect for a past king might encourage people to show disrespect for a living one. Nevertheless, it would certainly have been worthwhile for the king to prove that Arthur was a dead hero, not just one who was asleep and ready to return and claim his rightful throne at any moment.

Thus, the monks had many reasons for finding a grave for Arthur, even if one had never really existed in the first place. When the grave was allegedly discovered in 1192, a chronicler wrote that it was "surrounded with curtains" before the remains were removed. Was that to protect the sanctity of the dead, or to hide from prying eyes the fact that the monks were putting something into the grave first, before taking it out? We shall never know what really happened.

The monk Adam of Domerham reported that when the remains were moved in 1278, the skulls of the king and queen were placed on display "for the veneration of the people." For centuries it was customary to display the corpse of the king of England or France on top of his tomb before burial. In that way the common folk could assure themselves that the king was really dead. The display of skulls may have been carried out for the very same reason. No one could prove that one of the skulls definitely was that of King Arthur, but it would have made an impressive display in any case.

It is interesting to note that King Edward, who supervised the second reburial of Arthur's remains, came to Glastonbury shortly after a notable military victory over Welsh rebels. In his attention to the remains of the long-dead Arthur, he may have been placing psychological pressure on the restless Welsh. First, he was identifying himself with one of their national heroes and saying, in effect, that he was the legitimate heir to Arthur's power. Second, by displaying the remains he may have been reminding the Welsh, once again, that Arthur was really dead and would not return from Avalon to lead them out of their troubles. The message was clear: You had better accept things as they are.

There are quite a number of fairly conventional ghost stories connected with Arthur. For example, every Christmas Eve the ghost of Arthur is supposed to ride down what is called Chalice Hill in Glastonbury to drink from the miraculous spring at the bottom of the hill. His ghost is also reported at Tintagel Castle in Cornwall where, according to some legends, Arthur was born.

But it is not Arthur's ghost that we are interested in here. It is the still-alive, though sleeping, king that is our subject. And tales of this Arthur abound throughout the British Isles. This popular Welsh tale is typical:

A cattle drover named Dafyd Meirig cut a branch

from a yew tree to drive his cattle. This particular tree possessed magical properties. Branches from it could be used to point to gold or silver buried beneath the earth.

Accompanied by an English wizard, Dafyd went to the Welsh hill called Craig-y-Dinas, the Rock of the Fortress, where it was said that Arthur and his knights waited the call to fight again.

The yew stick directed Dafyd and his companion to a large flat stone in the ground. Beneath the stone was a narrow winding staircase that led to a passageway deep into the hillside. The two men followed it for several hundred yards, until the wizard touched Dafyd's sleeve and pointed to a heavy golden bell that hung at the end of the passage. They ducked beneath the bell and entered a cavern, lighted with an eerie glow.

Before them lay a thousand warriors, sleeping shoulder to shoulder, swords in hand. In the center sat the king, Arthur himself, motionless and obviously in a trance of some sort, clutching a massive broadsword. As Dafyd took in the scene, he realized that the light that seemed to come from a fire behind the king was cast by two huge heaps of gold. The magician told Dafyd that he could claim as much treasure as he could carry. The Welshman stuffed his shirt and coat with gold. The pair then left as they had come, taking great care to avoid the bell.

When they returned to the surface, they placed the stone back over the narrow opening. The magician then explained to Dafyd that he might return as often as he wished to get more gold, but he was warned never to disturb the bell.

Dafyd Meirig grew fat and lazy on the gold that he had carried out of the underground chamber that one night. It was years before he had the need, or could build up the courage, to enter the cave again —and this time alone. But after his gold finally ran out he could not bear to go back to work as a cattle drover. So he took a large sack and one night went back to the hillside and pushed aside the stone. Within a few moments he had filled the sack and, bowed down by the weight of the gold, he made his way back toward the passageway to the surface. But the sack was too large, and he couldn't bend low enough. The sack of gold struck the bell, which gave out an ear-splitting chime. Instantly every sleeping warrior in the chamber was awake and on his feet.

They grabbed Dafyd, beat him mercilessly, took the gold and threw him, empty-handed, into the night. After that, Dafyd never dared venture onto Craig-y-Dinas. But sitting in the tavern at night, he would often tell his story to others. The others searched the hill for the secret entrance, but no one was ever able to find it.

An eighteenth-century Scottish tale brings together

Arthur and his sleeping knights with the legendary magician and seer called Thomas the Rhymer.

A horse trader named Dick Canobie was traveling through the Scottish hills called Lucken Hare one night. This is an area that has associations both with Arthur and Thomas.

Dick met an imposing white-bearded old man, wearing a flowing cloak. The old man told the horse trader that he wished to buy some black horses and would pay a very good price for them. Dick sold the old man all the black horses he had. He was paid in gold coins with strange symbols and pictures on them. Strange or not, the gold was good, and Dick was well pleased with his bargain. The stranger then offered to buy more black horses the next month for the same price. Dick readily agreed.

The horse trader made several sales to the mysterious old man at Lucken Hare, always receiving the same kind of gold coins in payment. Finally, Dick became curious about his strange customer, and asked him where he lived, since there seemed to be no houses around. The old man tried to put him off. Dick persisted in his request, and the old man finally agreed to show the horse trader his home. But he said that Dick would see things that would test his courage, and if his courage failed the results might be disastrous for him.

Dick followed the old man up the slope of Lucken

Hare and to the entrance of a deep cave. The vast interior of the cave was lighted by flickering torches on the walls.

There was more to come, for carved into the walls of the cave were stalls, and in each stall stood a coal-black horse. At the foot of each stall lay a knight in coal-black armor. Both horse and knight appeared to be alive, but were unmoving.

At the center of the cave was a massive oaken table carved with mystic signs and symbols. On the table lay a sword and a hunting horn. The old man said, "Since you have been rash enough to intrude upon the realm of mystery and secret knowledge long forsaken and forgotten by the world of men, a choice is forced upon you. Either draw the sword or blow the horn. One or the other you must do. Choose correctly, you will reign here as king; chose badly and you forfeit your life. Trifle not with me, for I am Thomas the Rhymer."

Upon hearing the name of the famous magician, Dick knew that he was in serious trouble. Dick thought, what if the knights should awake and see him with a sword? It was better to first awaken them with the horn.

He blew the horn and the knights began to stir. The looks they gave him were not friendly. He grabbed the sword in order to defend himself, though against such a horde any fight would be hopeless. The magician had disappeared, but Dick could still hear his voice echoing through the cave: "Woe to the coward, that ever was born, who did not draw the sword, before he blew the horn."

The knights set upon the hapless man and beat him severely, then carried his nearly lifeless body out of the cave and dumped it on the hillside. He was found the next morning by shepherds who tried to help him, but it was too late. Dick lived only long enough to gasp out the story as it has been related here.

Clearly, these stories of King Arthur and Thomas the Rhymer take us into the realm of legend and fantasy. In different parts of Europe, similar tales have been told about Charlemagne, Frederick Barbarossa, and others. And they were often believed, particularly by people who were dissatisfied with the current ruler, and longed for the return of some hero from the past. These legends were powerful enough to generate genuine fear in some living rulers and produce real, if temporary, political effects.

About half a century before King Edward's very public reburial of what were supposed to be Arthur's remains, there had been a very disquieting sleeping hero incident in Europe. In 1204, Baldwin IX, Count of Flanders, was installed by the Crusaders as Emperor of Constantinople. Just what the Crusaders, who were supposed to be on their way to the Holy

Land to fight the Moslems, were doing trying to over-throw the Byzantine Emperor in Constantinople, who was a Christian, and was supposed to be the bulwark in the defense of Europe against a Moslem conquest, is a story for another day. In any case, this event captured the imagination of the people of Europe, who hated the Emperor at Constantinople almost as much as they hated the Moslems, perhaps more.

Baldwin's triumph was short-lived. Within a year he was captured and executed. However, back in Flanders, people refused to accept the fact that their count was dead. His death had taken place in a distant land, and they had seen no body displayed on the top of a tomb to confirm the fact of his death. As conditions in Flanders grew worse, stories concerning the survival of Baldwin began to circulate. It was said that he had not been killed at all, but had become a monk and was living in obscurity as a wandering beggar.

Twenty years after the death of Baldwin IX, a tall, bearded stranger walked out of the woods of Flanders near the city of Tournai. Whether he actually claimed to be Baldwin returned, or people just took him for that, is unclear, but whatever the circumstances, he began to play the role of Baldwin-returned and gathered a huge following. The pseudo-Baldwin became the focus of the common people's hopes and was regarded as nearly divine. People fought for a hair of his head or scrap of his clothing. They drank his bath water as if it were some sort of magic potion.

The impostor, for that is what this person turned out to be, was a man named Bertrand of Ray, who had served with the real Baldwin as a minstrel. Bertrand had spent years impersonating others before he fell into the highly successful role of the returned Baldwin. He wasn't particularly brave, for when his true identity was exposed, he ran away but soon set himself up in another town as Baldwin. Here, too, when threatened with exposure he fled. This time, he was captured, publicly confessed his impersonation, and was executed.

The fantasy, however, did not end with the execution of Bertrand of Ray. The common people continued to worship the memory of the impostor. In the words of a contemporary observer: "At Valenciennes, people await him [Baldwin] as the Britons await King Arthur."

The impostor had lived only six months between the time he announced that he was Baldwin and the time he was executed, but according to Professor Norman Cohn in his book *The Pursuit of the Millennium*: "Brief though the episode had been, it had inaugurated an epoch of social turbulence which was to continue for a century and a half."

A similar resurrection followed the death of the Holy Roman Emperor Frederick II in 1250. Frederick had an extraordinary, though short career. During his lifetime, there were many prophecies proclaiming that he was either the new Messiah or the Antichrist, depending on what opinion the prophet had of the Emperor. Frederick died suddenly without fulfilling either of these roles. So, once again, the rumors began to fly—Frederick was not dead, but merely sleeping in some distant and magical place.

Shortly after Frederick's death, an Italian monk reported that he had seen the Emperor descending into the crater of the volcano Mount Etna while a fiery army of knights fell hissing into the sea. The monk, who was hostile to Frederick, certainly meant to indicate that he had seen the Emperor going straight to Hell, but a lot of people did not take the statement that way. A few years later, an impostor appeared on the slopes of Mount Etna, claiming that he was the resurrected Frederick.

In 1284, thirty-four years after the death of the real Frederick, two different impostors appeared in different parts of Germany, claiming to be Frederick returned. Both abandoned the role when challenged. A third impostor, however, was made of sterner stuff. He appears to have been a madman who genuinely believed that he was Frederick. Like the pseudo-Baldwin, the pseudo-Frederick gathered a huge following, including a number of powerful princes. It may be that the princes did not believe in the resurrection of Frederick, but merely found it expedient to support the pretender for their own purposes.

Eventually this pretender, too, overreached himself. He was captured by his enemies and burned at the stake in Wetzlar, Germany, still claiming to be the returned emperor. "The method of execution is significant," notes Professor Cohn, "for burning was used not in cases of political insurrection but only in cases of sorcery or heresy."

Before going to the stake, the pseudo-Frederick promised that he would rise again within a few days. And sure enough, within a few days, another pretender appeared at Utrecht. He, too, was burned at the stake.

The pseudo-Frederick became almost as much of a legendary figure as the real Frederick. It was said that after his execution at Wetzlar, no bones were found in the ashes of the funeral pyre. This was taken to mean that his body had not been destroyed and that he would one day return again.

Such beliefs continued to circulate for centuries. In 1434, nearly two hundred years after the death of Frederick II, a chronicler wrote:

"From the Emperor Frederick, the heretic, a new heresy arose which some Christians still hold in secret; they believe absolutely that the Emperor Frederick is still alive and will remain alive until the end of the world, and that there has been and shall be no proper Emperor but he . . . The Devil invented this folly, so as to mislead these heretics and certain simple folk."

Just in case you think that sleeping hero beliefs are limited to medieval European peasants, or to people who live in distant and primitive parts of the world, consider this: Polls show that approximately 10 percent of the U.S. population believes that Elvis Presley is still alive.

6

▼ ▼

Never to Die

"He loves life; he dreads death;
He wills himself to live on."

There are those, fearing they will not be able to come back, decide they are not going.

The search for immortality—not immortal fame, or spiritual immortality, but physical immortality right here on this earth, or at least an extremely and unnaturally long life—is one that has been carried out from the dawn of human history. One of the best fictional treatments of the subject is in a short story by the mid-nineteenth-century writer, Edward Bulwer-Lytton. His story is called "The Haunters and the Haunted."

In the story the narrator finds evidence of a man who appears to have lived for centuries, under different identities, while hardly aging at all. Finally, he meets that man, who is going under the name Richards.

Richards explains to the narrator how certain individuals, with special powers, are able to prolong their lives, almost by an act of will:

"He loves life; he dreads death; *he wills himself to live on*. He cannot restore himself to youth; he cannot make himself immortal in the flesh and blood. But he may arrest, for a time so long as to appear incredible if I said it, that hardening of the parts that constitutes old age.

"A year may age him no more than an hour ages another. His intense will, scientifically trained into system operates, in short over the wear and tear of his own frame. He lives on. That he may not seem a portent and miracle, he *dies*, from time to time, seemingly, to certain persons. Having schemed the transfer of wealth that suffices to his wants, he disappears from one corner of the world, and contrives that the obsequies shall be celebrated.

"He reappears at another corner of the world, where he resides undetected, and does not visit the scenes of his former career till all who could remember his features are no more. He would be profoundly miserable if he had affections; he has none but himself. No good man would accept his longevity . . ."

While there are surprisingly few characters in fiction who are supposed to have discovered the secret of unnaturally long life like Bulwer-Lytton's Mr. Richards, there are several individuals who are really supposed to have lived for centuries. Of all the accounts of such individuals, the most credible is that of a fourteenth-century Frenchman and alchemist named Nicholas Flamel. As in the story of Victor Frankenstein, alchemy and the promise of physical immortality, or extremely long life, are closely associated.

What makes the story of Flamel so believable is that in many respects he was quite an ordinary and modest man. He was a scribe or notary—a man who prepared documents in an age when most people could not write. He lived in Paris, where he had a small but thriving business. He had married a wealthy woman named Pernelle, a few years older than himself, but by all accounts they were a devoted couple. Flamel had no particular interest in alchemy or other occult subjects.

Then one night he had a very strange dream. An angel gave him a book and said, "Flamel, look at this book. You will not in the least understand it, neither will anyone else; but a day will come when you will see in it something that no one else will see."

Flamel had almost forgotten the dream until 1357 when an unknown manuscript seller offered him the very book of which he had dreamed. It was a book filled with strange alchemical symbols and the words written in an ancient language that he could not understand. On the first leaf of the book there was a Latin inscription in gold letters, saying that the book was written by Abraham the Jew and that anyone who read it would be cursed "unless he were Sacrificer or Scribe."

As a scribe, Flamel felt safe from the curse. From the Latin inscription, which he could read, Flamel discovered that the book was an alchemical text that contained the formula used by the Jews to make gold to pay tribute to the Roman Empire. Unfortunately, as the dream had foretold, he could make absolutely nothing out of the rest of the manuscript. And the more he studied it, the less he understood.

He began making discreet inquiries among the many alchemists of Paris, and started his own modest alchemical experiments. He labored for twenty-one years without any success.

After that length of time, even the patient Flamel was getting discouraged. Suddenly he hit upon an idea. Since the book had been prepared by Abraham the Jew, perhaps there were Jews who could understand it. At that time, Spain was a center for Jewish scholarship. Flamel went to Spain and spent a year visiting Spanish synagogues, to no avail. Once again his efforts seemed to come to a dead end. But on his return journey to France, he met a Jewish scholar named Maitre Canches. Flamel had made copies of some of the drawings in the mysterious book and Maitre Canches immediately recognized them as coming from the *Ash Mezareph* of the Rabbi Abraham. This was a book that Jewish scholars thought had long been lost. Though Maitre Canches died before he actually had a chance to look at the book itself, he had given Flamel enough hints that he was able to work out the secrets for himself.

Flamel recorded that on January 7, 1382, he was able to change half a pound of lead into pure silver. He then went ahead to prepare the Great Elixir, and on April 25, he transmuted a half pound of lead into "pure gold, most certainly better than ordinary gold, being more soft and pliable."

Flamel wasn't greedy; he only accomplished this transmutation two more times in his life, and he continued to live in the same frugal, pious manner as before. His beloved wife died in 1397, and Flamel spent the rest of his life writing about alchemy and doing good works. When he died on March 22, 1417, he left behind a notable record of endowments to churches, hospitals, and other charitable institutions.

Since Flamel seemed to have so much more wealth than he would have acquired working as a scribe, people assumed that his story about having made gold must be true. What else, they reasoned, could possibly account for his wealth? After his death, neighbors ransacked Flamel's property looking for "the secret." They didn't find it, but two centuries later, people were still searching the land he had owned and still without any success.

All very interesting, you say, but what has it to do with immortality? To the extent that people know of alchemy today, it is thought of as an old and foolish attempt to turn lead or some other base metal into gold. That's true, as far as it goes, but for centuries the alchemical quest was a great deal more than that.

Explaining just exactly what else, however, is nearly impossible. The practice, indeed the obsession with alchemy, lasted for centuries. It existed in many societies and at all stations in life. Simply, it was an attempt to find the basis, the essence, of all things—of matter and even of life itself. A feature of alchemy was its secrecy and obscurity. Alchemists cloaked their activities in symbolic pictures and coded language. An alchemical text that no one could understand, like the one described in the Flamel story, was not uncommon. Some alchemists seemed to fear that if they wrote in plain language their "secrets" would be stolen, or would fall into the hands of the unworthy. Others were afraid that full knowledge of their activities might gain them unwelcome attention from civil or religious authorities. And there were plenty of downright alchemical frauds who possessed no secrets, but hid their nonsense under a load of impressive-looking symbols and obscure language.

At the end of the alchemical quest was a substance called, among other things, "the Elixir of Life" or the "philosophers' stone." The elixir was supposed to confer, if not actual immortality, then at least an unnaturally long life to anyone who took it.

Since Flamel was thought to have found the answer to one big alchemical question—how to make gold from base metal—many believed that he had also found that other great alchemical goal, the Elixir of Life.

This is a claim that Flamel himself never made. Nicholas Flamel's death seems to be fairly well supported by evidence. He left a very detailed will, which still exists. Even his tombstone has been found, though it was found in someone's house, not in a cemetery. Still, the belief grew that Flamel, like Bulwer-Lytton's character Richards, faked his own death and went into hiding. Unlike the fictional Richards, however, Flamel did have "affections" for his wife, Pernelle. She too was given the elixir and her death was faked years before Flamel's. She then went off to some distant place to prepare the way for Flamel's own disappearance. They were reportedly seen alive and well in India in the seventeenth century. By the mid-eighteenth century the pair apparently felt that they had been away from their original home long enough, and would no longer be recognized. But they were recognized from drawings when they attended the opera in Paris. They had hardly aged at all in four hundred years.

They have not been seen recently.

While Nicholas Flamel was a modest and retiring man, the same cannot be said for the Count de Saint-Germain. He was both a flamboyant and mysterious character, who attracted attention wherever he went. No one knows who he really was or where he came from. The title he went by was fraudulent, as he sometimes admitted.

The first record of him comes from 1745 when he was arrested as a spy in England. Horace Walpole noted in a letter:

". . . the other day they seized an odd man who goes by the name of the Count Saint-Germain. He has been here these two years and will not tell who he is, or whence he came . . . He sings, plays the violin wonderfully, composes, is mad, and not very sensible. He is called an Italian, a Spaniard, a Pole, a somebody that married a great fortune in Mexico, and ran away with her jewels to Constantinople; a priest, a fiddler, a vast nobleman . . ."

Some ten years later, this "odd man" turned up in Paris, and quickly became a popular figure among the aristocracy. He claimed that he lived completely off a mysterious elixir, which he is supposed to have sold at an enormous price. He would sit through elegant dinner parties without touching a morsel of food or a drop of wine, saying he did not need such nourishment or stimulation. Quite soon, the most incredible stories about him began to make the rounds of Parisian society. At one dinner party, so it was said, Saint-Germain was speaking with easy familiarity of King Richard the Lionhearted and some of the conversations they had while in Palestine together during the Crusades. When some of the other guests were openly skeptical, Saint-Germain turned to his valet, who was standing behind his chair, and asked him to confirm the truth of the story.

"I really cannot say, sir," the servant replied. "You forget, sir, I have only been five hundred years in your service!"

"Ah! True," said Saint-Germain. "I remember now—it was a little before your time."

A friend and confidant of the powerful Madame de Pompadour wrote:

"A man who was as amazing as a witch came often . . . This was the Count de Saint-Germain, who wished to make people believe that he lived for several centuries. One day Madame said to him . . . 'What sort of a man was Francis I . . . ?' 'A good sort of fellow' said Saint-Germain, 'too fiery—I could have given him a useful piece of advice but he would not have listened.' He then described in very general terms the beauty of Mary Stuart and La Reine Margot. 'You seem to have seen them all . . .' 'Sometimes,' said Saint-Germain, 'I amuse myself, not by making people believe, but by letting them believe that I have lived from time immemorial.' "

Pompadour complained, "But you do not tell us your age, and yet you pretend you are very old. The Countess de Gergy, who was, I believe, ambassadress at Vienna some fifty years ago, says she saw you there exactly the same as you now appear."

"That is true, Madame," replied Saint-Germain. "I knew Madame de Gergy many years ago."

"But according to her account, you must be more than a hundred years old."

"That is not impossible, but it is much more possible that the good lady is in her dotage."

When Pompadour pressed Saint-Germain to give the King some of the Elixir of Life that he was reputed to possess, he replied, "Oh Madame, the physicians would have me broken on the wheel, were I to think of drugging his majesty."

It sounds very much as if Saint-Germain was playing a little game, of not quite admitting he was immortal, but not quite denying it either. It was part of his charm and fascination.

Another adventurer, Casanova, met Saint-Germain on several occasions. He wrote in his *Memoirs*: "This extraordinary man, intended by nature to be the king of the impostors and quacks, would say in an easy and assured manner that he was three hundred years old, that he knew the secrets of universal medicine, that he possessed a mastery over nature, that he could melt diamonds . . . Notwithstanding his boastings, his bare-faced lies and his manifold eccentricities, I cannot say I thought him offensive."

Some of the more outrageous stories attributed to Saint-Germain may not have been his doing at all. At one point, the king's foreign minister, the Duc de Choiseul, who disliked and distrusted Saint-Germain, hired an impostor to impersonate the man in the salons of Paris in an attempt to discredit him. It may have been a case of an impostor impersonating an impostor, and it all becomes very confusing. This second Saint-Germain went around making truly absurd claims, such as having been a close friend of Saint Anne, the mother of the Virgin Mary, and making remarks like "I always knew Christ would come to a bad end." These were the sort of comments that could get you in really serious trouble.

Ultimately, it was politics, not any claims for immortality, that did get Saint-Germain in trouble and made it necessary for him to leave France permanently around 1670. From that time onward, stories of his comings and goings are vague and unreliable. It was rumored that he was in London, in St. Petersburg, and in Germany. He seems to have spent his final days in the court of his friend, the Prince of Hesse Cassel, dying there in the year 1782.

Or did he? Almost immediately upon reports of his death there were other rumors that he had never really died. How could he? This was the man who possessed the Elixir of Life!

A journal published in 1783—a year after Saint-Germain was said to have died—said he was expected to return soon. Madame de Genlis was convinced that she had seen him in Vienna in 1821. In 1836, a volume of *Souvenirs* by the Countess d'Adhemar, who claimed to be familiar with the Court at Versailles in the last days of the French monarchy, insisted that she had seen Saint-Germain as late as 1793, and that he warned her about the death of Queen Marie Antoinette. He told her that she would see him five more times "and do not wish for a sixth," and she claims that she saw him five times between then and 1820.

In 1845, Franz Graffer declared in his *Memoirs* that he met Saint-Germain and was told that the Count would appear in the Himalayas toward the turn of the century. What this creature of the elegant salons of Paris had to do with the Himalayas is unclear, but around the turn of the last century, a variety of occultists who had become fascinated by Eastern mysticism insisted that they had indeed seen the Count in Tibet or other places in the Orient. He had now become one of the immortal "ascended masters" or "secret masters" that form such an important part of occult lore.

In the 1930s, the Count was reported to have put in an appearance on California's Mount Shasta, in one of his strangest incarnations. He became one of the principal figures in the once-thriving "I AM" cult founded by a Kansas swindler named Guy Warren Ballard and his wife, a former vaudeville performer and clerk in an occult bookstore. One thing the Ballards really hated was President Franklin D. Roosevelt and his wife. They tried to destroy the first family with what they called "Saint-Germain's Blue Ray." Followers of the Ballards would sit around and shout in unison "Blast! Blast! Blast!" It didn't work. Ballard died in 1939, but his wife and son were still trying to sell immortality by mail for years. They were finally convicted of fraud, and the cult disappeared.

As late as January, 1972, a young man called Richard Chanfray appeared on French television claiming that he was Saint-Germain and that he was able to transform lead into gold, using only a camping stove.

Saint-Germain had become a model that was to be emulated by other, less successful adventurers. Foremost among these was the man who called himself the Count Allendro de Cagliostro. While Saint-

Germain's origins remain unknown, Cagliostro was almost certainly a Sicilian swindler, and possibly a murderer named Joseph Balsamo.

Balsamo and his wife, styling themselves the Count and Countess of Cagliostro, traveled throughout Europe, telling fortunes, selling alchemical secrets, communing with the spirits, and doing whatever itinerant magicians of the day had to do to make a living. They moved rapidly from place to place, often barely one step ahead of their creditors or the law. In fact, Cagliostro did wind up in jail in England after claiming he knew the "secret" for picking winning lottery tickets.

It wasn't until the couple reached Paris that their career really took off. Cagliostro said that he met Saint-Germain and was initiated into all the "mysteries" presided over by that mysterious figure. It is not at all certain that Cagliostro ever even met Saint-Germain, but Saint-Germain's reputation was so powerful that it was extremely useful to pretend that there was an association.

Cagliostro founded his own secret society, based on what he called Egyptian Freemasonry. According to Cagliostro, the secrets of Egyptian Freemasonry had first been revealed to the biblical prophets Enoch and Elias, but the system had been much debased until he rediscovered its original secrets. Cagliostro promised that those who became disciples of his society would be led to perfection by means of physical and moral regeneration. They would be returned to that state of perpetual youth, beauty, and innocence that mankind had been deprived of by original sin. His formula for eternal life was a curious mixture of magical theory and the medical practices of the eighteenth century.

While Cagliostro was riding high in public favor in Paris, he was implicated in a complex plot to steal a diamond necklace under the ruse that it was being purchased by Queen Marie Antoinette. Cagliostro and his wife spent months in the Bastille before ever coming to trial.

In the trial both were acquitted, but they were also banished from France and forced to leave behind most of the wealth that they had accumulated. Fleeing to England, Cagliostro is supposed to have angrily predicted the outbreak of the French Revolution and the doom of those who persecuted him. He was urged by his friends to warn the King and Queen of their fate, but Cagliostro said they would not believe him, and besides, there was no way to change what was predestined. This account, which has been repeated hundreds of times, would be quite remarkable, if we could be sure it was true. Unfortunately, the story of Cagliostro's prediction of the French Revolution was told only *after* the French Revolution had actually taken place. But the mere fact the tale has been told so often, and believed by so many, is a good indication of Cagliostro's enduring reputation as a wonder worker.

If Cagliostro could indeed predict the future, he should have taken a closer look at his own future. In 1791, he turned up in Rome and tried to start a lodge of his Egyptian Freemasons. At the time, the Roman Catholic Church was fiercely opposed to Freemasonry, and to attempt to practice its most exotic form practically in the shadow of the Vatican was an act of rashness that bordered on the insane. Cagliostro was charged with being a Freemason, a heretic, and a sorcerer, and was condemned to death. Ultimately, his sentence was commuted to one of perpetual imprisonment in the Castle St. Angelo. After an unsuccessful escape attempt, he was moved to the fortress of San Leo, where he was placed in a tiny rock-cut dungeon, and he died there. It was a bad end.

But to many occultists, Cagliostro is not a swindler and scoundrel, but a hero, and a man in possession of genuine "secrets," including the secret of nearly eternal life. The claim has often been made that he actually did escape from Castle St. Angelo and lived on. Along with Saint-Germain, he is regarded as one of those Hidden Masters, who reappear from time to time, to impart their wisdom to the select few. While Cagliostro has never been as popular as Saint-Germain, sightings of him alive and well in Tibet,

Paris, and California have been reported through the centuries.

Whether Flamel, Saint-Germain, and Cagliostro ever discovered the Elixir of Life is, to put the best face on it, an open question. While we don't know whether they are still alive, we do know that they once lived. With Fulcanelli, we don't even know that.

The mystery of the "Immortal Fulcanelli" is a twentieth-century mystery. It began in Paris in the fall of 1926, with the publication of a little book called *The Mystery of the Cathedrals*. The author was known only by the name Fulcanelli. He said he was an alchemist, and that his book was written only for fellow alchemists. It must have been, for certainly no one else could understand it. The book claimed that the great Gothic cathedrals of Europe were really "stone books." The author stated that if the structures and measurements of the cathedrals were properly understood, they would reveal the secrets of alchemy. A mere three hundred copies of this strange, obscure, and quite incomprehensible volume were printed. But in spite of this, and perhaps because of it, the book gained quite a reputation among French occultists. There was particular fascination with Fulcanelli. Who was this man of mystery, people wondered.

The only clue to the identity of the author was a

man calling himself "Eugene Canseliet," who wrote a preface to the book. He said that Fulcanelli is "his Master," but having achieved the "Pinnacle of Knowledge" had disappeared in 1922. "Fulcanelli is no more."

The Fulcanelli mystery certainly didn't end there. It became one of the central themes of a book called *The Morning of the Magicians*, first published in France in 1960. One of the coauthors of the book, Jacques Bergier, claimed that in 1937 he met a mysterious alchemist, whose real name he never learned. "The man of whom we are speaking disappeared some time ago without leaving any visible traces, to lead a clandestine existence, having severed all connection between himself and the century in which he lived." The author speculates that this was really the man who called himself Fulcanelli. *The Morning of the Magicians* was a huge best-seller in Europe and was very popular and influential among the occult-minded in the United States as well. It has been credited with sparking a revival of interest in occultism that took place in the 1960s. It certainly helped to keep the story of the semi-immortal adept, who would appear and then disappear regularly throughout history, alive.

This mysterious figure, who may (or may not) have been Fulcanelli, told Berger about the power of atomic energy, and this was supposed to have happened well before the rest of the world knew about it. He revealed that the civilization of the lost continent of Atlantis had been destroyed by atomic radiation. The mystery man also told Berger that the Great Secret of alchemy is rediscovered by a few men every century.

Then, in a 1971 English translation of the book that started it all, Canseliet revealed that he had seen Fulcanelli again nearly thirty years after his disappearance in 1922. Canseliet stated that in the early 1950s, he received a summons from his Master to meet him in a chateau in the mountains. When he arrived, he was surprised to discover that Fulcanelli, who had been about eighty in 1922, looked thirty years younger.

While many have called the alchemical substance that confers near immortality the Elixir of Life, another common term, and the one used most often in the Fulcinelli story, is the Philosophers' Stone. After the Stone is created, in what is called the Great Work or the Master Work, the alchemist swallows a small bit of it twice a year. He then loses all his hair, his nails, and his teeth, but they grow again stronger and healthier than before. The adept grows younger, and no longer needs food, though he may eat for enjoyment, or simply to disguise the fact that he has discovered the Great Secret.

Now all of this gets pretty deep and pretty

confusing—deliberately so. It is really hopeless to try and sort it all out. It is also rather pointless to insist that the stories of Fulcinelli, Saint-Germain, and all the others who are rumored to have found the secret of physical immortality and live on amongst us, are full of contradictions and have absolutely no solid evidence to back them up. To those who really believe in such individuals—and there are hundreds of thousands of people who do believe—physical reality is irrelevant. If you believe it, that's good enough.

It is this state of mind that keeps tales of the immortal masters living undetected among us circulating even now, as the twentieth century draws to a close, and even though the theory of alchemy was supposed to have been thrown into history's wastebasket centuries ago. The lure of immortality makes the tale almost impossible to throw away.

But immortality is not always a desirable state. There are legends which hold that it can also be a great curse. One of the most persistent of these is the legend of the Wandering Jew.

The legend can be traced back to the early seventeenth century, though it is probably much older than that. In 1602, a pamphlet appeared in Germany which said that in 1547 the Lutheran bishop of Schleswig had once met a Jew named Ahasuerus in the city of Hamburg and learned that he was fifteen centuries old. According to the tale, the man had been a cobbler in Jerusalem at the time of Christ. He turned Christ away from his door and, because of that, had been cursed to wander from place to place until the Second Coming. The origin of the pamphlet is unknown. The bishop who was supposed to have met Ahasuerus was long dead before it was published. Whatever its origins, the legend became enormously popular, and was retold in different versions throughout Europe. In some versions the Wandering Jew was a villain, in others a tragic figure, while in still others he was given almost heroic stature.

What kept the legend going was other reports of meetings with the eternal wanderer. Besides his Hamburg appearance, he is said to have been recognized in Spain in 1575, Vienna in 1599, Ypres in 1623, Brussels in 1640, and Paris in 1644; and at various other places, mostly in Central Europe at various other dates in the seventeenth century.

Some of these reports were doubtless just made up, while others may have been inspired by impostors. Later appearances are less common, although they include Newcastle in England in 1790, and one in Salt Lake City in 1868, when the wanderer met a Mormon named O'Grady. The event was duly reported in *The Deseret News*.

There were some earlier legends of individuals—in this case Romans—who had insulted Christ and were condemned to a life of eternal wandering. There is even a Buddhist legend of Pindola, an unworthy follower of the Buddha, who was condemned to be unable to die. But none of these legends ever attained the popularity of the story of the Wandering Jew. It has been the basis for plays, poems, and stories right up to the present day.

7

▼ ▼

The Body Snatchers

"Burke's the butcher, Hare's the thief"

We don't know for certain, but we assume that Victor Frankenstein got the bits and pieces with which he created his monster by stealing bodies from graveyards in the dead of night.

At one point, Victor says, "Darkness had no effect upon my fancy; and the churchyard was to me merely the receptacle of bodies deprived of life."

Many of the Frankenstein films contain a good gloomy cemetery scene in which Ygor, or some other crazed and deformed assistant, is digging up a body for his boss. Such scenes were by no means just a product of the filmmaker's imagination. Stealing bodies from graveyards was at one time a fairly common practice. Those who plied the trade of stealing corpses were called "body snatchers," given the ironic title of "resurrectionists," or the more accurate one of "sack-'em-up men."

The business of body snatching grew out of a clash between religion and tradition and science. In Europe it had long been traditional to bury the bodies of the dead with great care and reverence. If someone wanted to know what the human body looked like inside, the proper thing to do was consult books written by the ancient Romans and Greeks. These contained a wealth of misinformation, but people didn't care.

However, there were those inquisitive individuals, like Leonardo da Vinci, who didn't trust the ancient authorities and wanted to see for themselves. Leonardo personally dissected some thirty corpses. By the middle of the seventeenth century, the importance of basing the study of anatomy on the dissection of human cadavers was firmly established throughout much of Europe.

In the British Isles, and particularly in Scotland, however, the atmosphere was quite different. There was a strong belief that on Judgment Day the physical body as well as the soul would be resurrected. Thus, if a body was dissected, the individual's chances for eternal life would be imperiled.

So long as the few physicians that practiced learned their anatomy from ancient books, this belief created no particular problems. But as the number of physicians grew, and the study of human anatomy became an increasingly important part of the training of physicians, conflict inevitably arose.

Until the end of the seventeenth century, the only corpses legally available for dissection in Scotland were those of people who had died on the gallows. Edinburgh surgeons were restricted to one body a year for dissection. The body was usually divided into ten parts and distributed to the students to work on.

Even with these limitations, there were problems. While the public had no objection to executions—indeed they turned out in huge numbers to witness public hangings—they had a genuine horror of having the bodies of even the most notorious criminals turned over to the anatomists. Dissection was considered "a fate worse than death." The relatives and friends of the condemned were ready to move heaven and earth to keep their bodies from falling into the hands of the surgeons. As often as not, those who had turned out to cheer the hanging were ready to help protect the body of the hanged.

The condemned themselves were haunted by the fear of "miracle revivals," that is, that they would be cut down from the gallows before they were completely dead and "come back to life" on the dissection table.

There were scores of stories of such revivals, and

some of them may even have been true. "Half-Hangit" Maggie Dickson was supposed to have been executed in Edinburgh in 1728. After she was cut down, a group of medical students tried to spirit her body away, but they were fought off by her relatives and the mob that had turned out to witness the hanging.

Maggie's relatives put her coffin in a horse-drawn wagon for the nine-mile trip back home. Along the bumpy road the jolting of the cart shook the unconscious, but not yet dead, Maggie "back to life." Not only did she recover from her execution, she lived to a ripe old age and had a large number of children. "Half-Hangit" Maggie was a source of local pride, and the townsfolk often pointed her out to visitors.

On the other hand, from Germany came the story of a notorious murderer who had just been hanged, but who began to show signs of life on the dissection table. The surgeon in charge of the dissection noted that, with proper attention, the man could probably be returned to life. "But when it is considered what a rascal we should again have among us, that he was hanged for so cruel a murder, and that if we should restore him to life he would probably kill somebody else, I say, gentlemen, all these things considered, it is my opinion that we had better proceed with the dissection."

They did.

With tales like these to prey on their already gloomy minds, there can be little doubt that many of the condemned would have echoed the sentiments of the Smithfield butcher who, when arrested after stabbing his wife, shouted: "I have killed the best wife in the world, and I am certain of being hanged, but for God's sake don't let me be anatomized!"

Though hangings were reasonably common events, the gallows could not supply nearly enough corpses to meet the requirements of the growing number of medical students. Doctors sought, and sometimes obtained, permission to dissect the bodies of those who died in the poorhouse. In 1694, the doctors of Edinburgh were granted "those bodies that dye in the correction house, the bodies of foundlings who dye betwixt the tyme that they are weaned and their being put to schools or trades . . ." In those days people were not sentimental about the children of the poor.

But even this boon did not increase the supply of corpses sufficiently to meet the demand. By the beginning of the nineteenth century, there were nearly one thousand medical students in Edinburgh alone. In order to train their students properly, the anatomists had to supply them with fresh corpses for dissection and training, and thus had to turn with increasing frequency to the services of those who were not too squeamish to steal bodies.

Much of the body-snatching activity was carried

out by medical students themselves. Usually the students were far from wealthy, and training with a good professor of anatomy stretched their meager budgets to the breaking point. By helping to supply their professors with anatomical subjects, they were able to cut the cost of their own education. In certain medical societies and schools throughout the British Isles, body snatching, or at least keeping silent about the body-snatching activities of others, was a requirement of membership or admission.

A group of prominent London physicians who had once worked in Scotland sent a letter of advice to their colleagues in Aberdeen, Scotland, noting that dissection was being neglected. "We are certain that proper subjects might be easily had there, and will certainly be had, unless students are wanting themselves in spirited exertion or in common prudence. Bodies are procured in London for dissection almost every day. We leave anyone to form their own opinion whether it would not be an easier affair at Aberdeen."

This was a clear invitation to body snatching. The prominent physicians considered it a worthwhile activity. The medical students who engaged in the practice were young, daring, and like Victor Frankenstein, outspokenly unafraid of the terrors of the graveyard.

Not all medical students were as free from "superstitious terrors" as Victor Frankenstein. There are records of fines being levied by medical schools upon those who were unwilling to do their part in obtaining corpses. Others paid for substitutes to take their place on the raids.

There was a real danger involved. Being apprehended by the law was the least part of it, for the fines were usually light, and were often paid by the medical school or society. Far more worrisome was the danger of falling into the hands of a mob of angry relatives and townsfolk. Though there is no evidence that a resurrectionist was ever killed on the spot by a mob, medical students and other body snatchers were occasionally beaten, sometimes severely, when caught.

And then there is a story about a group of students who were raiding an isolated Scottish graveyard when they heard approaching voices and quickly fled. Two farmhands happened to be passing and, looking over the graveyard wall, they saw the open grave, with the corpse already half out.

Assuming that the students would return soon to collect their prize, the farmhands removed and hid the corpse, and one of them took its place. Sure enough, the students came back and one of them whispered, "C'mon boys, give me a hand with him," From the grave came the reply, "Let be, lads, I'll raise myself." That particular body-snatching raid ended abruptly.

The professional body snatchers were generally social outcasts, men who were so far down in society that they would do a job that was despised by practically everyone else. Most were heavy drinkers, who had failed at other jobs. Often they had begun as gravediggers, but had been unable to hold even that lowly job. And yet some of their number were surprisingly skilled at the business of grave robbing and they often worked in close association with respected medical men. While there is no record of any professional body snatcher becoming rich, it could provide a regular income.

Edinburgh's leading body snatcher, Andrew Merrilees, popularly known as Merry Andrew, gained a measure of fame in his profession by selling his own sister's corpse to the anatomists.

Most body-snatching raids were carefully planned. For a raid to be really successful, no clues could be left to show that the grave had ever been tampered with in the first place. If people knew a grave had been robbed, the atmosphere could become extremely uncomfortable for any nearby medical schools. Once a graveyard was found to have been disturbed, guards were often posted, thus cutting off a potential source of supply.

Planning for a robbery began as soon as the robbers got word that a funeral was going to take place. To get the information they needed, they might send a spy, someone dressed in mourning clothes, to mingle with the real mourners. (One member of a gang of professional body snatchers attended so many funerals he was called "Praying Howard.") Or the gang might bribe a church warden or gravedigger to get the necessary information: what the layout of the graveyard was, how deep the coffin was buried, what sort of coffin it was, and whether any traps had been set to foil the robbers.

Body snatchers almost always worked at night, though at extremely isolated graveyards they might even carry out their activities in the daytime. Actually digging up a grave was not as hard as you might imagine. Since only fresh burials were robbed, old rotted corpses being of no value to the anatomist, the robbers were working in earth that was not hard-packed. And the coffins of the poor were generally buried only four feet beneath the ground, rather than the traditional six. In times of epidemic or famine, several coffins were often piled in a single grave.

Rather than exposing the coffin completely, the body snatchers cleared only the head half. The lid was then broken with a crowbar, and the corpse was hauled out by means of ropes or hooks. Most coffins were made entirely of wood. Generally, the body was stripped and the clothes were put back in the grave. If apprehended, the robbers did not want to be accused of stealing the clothes in addition to snatching the body.

The careful robbers shoveled the dirt onto a canvas

sheet and, when the operation was over, dumped the dirt back into the hole, and as closely as possible returned the grave to its previous appearance. If luck was with them, the robbery would never be detected.

Almost as necessary for the job as a spade was a large sack—hence the name, "sack-'em-up men." The body was placed in a sack. It was clearly undesirable to be seen driving around the countryside with a corpse in your wagon. It was also unwise to go directly from the graveyard to the back of a medical school. Even in a sack, a body makes an easily identifiable bundle. Body snatchers usually hid their prize in an abandoned house or some other out-of-the-way place where it could be picked up later.

One of those respectable medical men, who regularly cooperated with the body snatchers, was Robert Liston of Edinburgh, who was to become one of Europe's leading surgeons. Liston was a man of great physical strength, a considerable asset for a surgeon in the days before anesthesia, when amputations had to be performed on screaming, struggling patients. Liston's surgical prowess earned him a place in the *Guinness Book of Records*, which credits him with performing the fastest amputation of a limb in the pre-anesthetic era. It took a mere thirty-three seconds to amputate a patient's leg. Unfortunately, during his record-breaking feat he accidentally amputated three of his assistant's fingers. Liston's admiring colleagues said of him that when he amputated, "the gleam of the knife was followed so instantaneously by the sound of the sawing as to make the two actions appear almost simultaneous."

Robert Liston was obviously not a squeamish man, nor was he a man to do things by halves. When he went looking for bodies to dissect, he took as his associate the notorious Ben Crouch, the "Corpse King" of London. Forced to flee his native city, Crouch became the Edinburgh physician's chief assistant and unofficial instructor in the art of body snatching.

Liston's body-snatching exploits were nearly as legendary as his surgical skill. Once, it was said, Liston led a party of students into an Edinburgh graveyard to dig up a number of freshly buried corpses. The gang had dug up two corpses, and were trying for a third when suddenly an angry mob, some armed with shotguns, descended upon them. The brawny Liston, toting a corpse under each arm, made his escape through a door in the graveyard wall and lay hidden in a ditch for hours with his two dead companions.

On another occasion, it was said that Liston and Ben Crouch entered a graveyard at midnight, only to find that they had been preceded by not one but two rival gangs of resurrectionists. The two gangs were arguing over the ownership of a corpse. Instead of joining the argument, the surgeon, dressed in black, hid himself behind a nearby tombstone, and then jumped up suddenly with a hideous scream. That was enough to frighten even other body snatchers. They fled, leaving the field and the corpse to Liston and Crouch.

The best and easiest way to get a body was to steal it before it was buried, and this is just what many of the body snatchers did. Undertakers were often bribed to turn over bodies to the resurrectionists, and bury something other than the body in the coffin. Thus, the undertaker could collect twice on one burial, and no one was the wiser.

The body snatchers not only kept up on the news of who had died, but were well-informed about who was about to die, particularly people who were poor and alone and were not likely to have anyone to see to the proper care of their corpse. Often members of the resurrectionists gang would appear at a poor lodging house, posing as the relatives of a recently deceased lodger. They would carry off the body before the real relatives, if any, came around. No doubt the claiming of bodies by bogus relatives was often made easier by an exchange of coin between the resurrectionists and the unscrupulous lodging house owner.

Resurrectionists, much like vultures, would hover around the dying, waiting for the right moment to strike. It's not hard to imagine how some of the body snatchers waiting around for a subject to die, might

have been sorely tempted to cut short the sufferings
of the dying, along with his own waiting. As noted,
most of the professional body snatchers were heavy
drinkers, and products of a world where sudden and
violent death was common. A fresh body brought to
the side door of an anatomical laboratory in the middle of the night would be paid for in cold cash—no
questions asked. The cash could provide the price for
a desperately needed bottle. There was a genuine fear
that body snatchers might turn murderers.

In Scotland, parents warned their children away
from dark and isolated streets with tales of body
snatchers crouched in the shadows with chloroform
pad and sack, ready to pounce on the unsuspecting
pedestrian.

One part of the city of Glasgow, a narrow network
of dark and sinister alleys and passageways called the
Old Whynd, had a particularly persistent reputation
as the haunt of murderously inclined body snatchers,
though there is no record of anyone ever actually
having been murdered there by body snatchers. It just
looked like a place where such attacks could happen.
Long after the era of body snatching had passed, city
residents would clap their hands over their mouths
when they passed the Old Whynd. Many no longer
remembered, if they had ever known, that the custom
first began with the belief that a hand over the mouth
would keep the chloroform from taking effect.

Though murderous body snatchers were nowhere near as common in real life as they were in popular legend, that does not mean that such things never happened. And one case transformed a general fear of body snatching into full-blown hysteria. It is the case of a pair whose names are still notorious throughout the English-speaking world—Burke and Hare.

William Burke and William Hare were both originally from Ireland. They arrived in Edinburgh, where they were to become so well known, by different routes and at different times. Burke had abandoned a family in Ireland and in Scotland took up with a woman named Helen McDougal.

In 1827, Burke and McDougal found themselves in Edinburgh living in a squalid lodging house owned by William Hare and his common-law wife. It was located in a part of Edinburgh called the West Port, a poor section of foul-smelling streets and closes (narrow passageways) that had a bad reputation long before Burke and Hare began their operations.

Burke and Hare were never professional resurrectionists. They never robbed a grave. They got into the body-selling business almost by accident. Another of Hare's lodgers, an old soldier, died owing the landlord £4 in back rent. Hare got the bright idea of selling the old soldier's body to a surgeon. But he needed some help, so he enlisted Burke's aid. The pair pried open the coffin into which the parish undertaker had nailed the old soldier, and replaced the body with a sack of tanner's bark.

On the night of November 20, 1827, Burke and Hare delivered their merchandise to the laboratory of Dr. Robert Knox at Number 10 Surgeon's Square, next to the Royal Medical Society. They received £7 for their delivery, and no questions were asked. Burke later claimed they "were always encouraged to get more."

But with or without encouragement, the pair had discovered a way to make quick and easy money. Of course, they couldn't count on somebody dying of natural causes in Hare's lodging house every day. Another sick lodger was a man named Joseph. But he clung stubbornly to life until Burke and Hare became impatient and smothered him. This time they got £10 for the corpse and decided to expand their activities.

They began luring people to Hare's lodging house with the promise of a drink. When the potential victim was intoxicated, Burke, the stronger of the pair, would generally smother him. The body would then be packed into a sack or a tea chest and delivered to Dr. Knox, who was delighted by the freshness of the corpses that Burke and Hare were providing. As usual, no questions were asked about the source.

Most of Burke and Hare's victims were old, poor, and friendless, the sort whose sudden disappearance would attract little, if any, notice. Newcomers to town were the most frequent victims. In his confession, Burke described the victims as "first ae drunk auld wife, and then anither drunk auld wife, and then a third drunk auld wife, and then a drunk auld or sick man or twa."

Even after Burke and Hare were apprehended and had confessed their crimes, the police were unable to discover the names of several of their victims. They had been killed and dissected, and not a living soul had missed them.

Nine months after the pair committed their first murder, they were finally caught as a result of their own carelessness. Actually, they had been careless all along. Burke recalled walking through the street with a sack slung over his back while a crowd of children followed behind chanting, "He's carrying a body. He's carrying a body." Only the fact that the police were ineffective, and not very interested in the fate of the poor, made it possible for Burke and Hare to get away with their crimes as long as they did.

Finally, the pair became so careless even the Edinburgh police couldn't overlook them. In late October, 1828, a couple of guests dropped over to Burke's room. The room was empty because Burke had gone out to buy some whiskey, but the guests looked around and found the corpse of one Madgy Docherty under a pile of straw. They reported their discovery to the authorities, and eventually constables came to search Burke's room. They didn't find a body, but did find a pile of blood-stained clothes.

Burke and Helen McDougal were arrested immediately. Hare and his wife were arrested the next day, and the police searched Dr. Knox's laboratory. There, in a tea chest, was Docherty's corpse.

When everything is totaled up, Burke and Hare were found to have been responsible for providing sixteen murdered people for Dr. Knox's anatomy classes. Up close, the entire case is squalid, sad, and rather commonplace. But like the Jack the Ripper case a half century later, this one captured public attention, and over the years it has retained its air of gloomy and grisly fascination.

After Burke and Hare were arrested, the authorities thought the best way to insure a conviction was to offer one his freedom if he would testify against the other. Burke was the likeliest prospect for a guilty verdict, and a formidable case could be made against him and McDougal. Hare was persuaded to give evidence against his former associates.

The case created an enormous sensation in the newspapers. When the trial opened, on Christmas Eve, it seemed as if everybody in Edinburgh tried to jam into the courtroom. The trial ran for twenty-four straight hours. In the end, Burke was convicted, as expected. Helen McDougal, however, was acquitted for lack of evidence. "Nelly, you are out of the scrape," the judge told her.

The final irony, of course, is that Burke's body was ordered turned over to the anatomists for dissection. The judge told Burke, "I trust that if it is ever customary to preserve skeletons, yours will be preserved in order that posterity may keep in remembrance your atrocious crimes."

So, in the end, William Burke alone suffered legal punishment for the series of atrocious murders. The Hares and McDougal, who were principals or accessories in the crimes, went free, though they were nearly lynched by mobs after the trial.

And what of Dr. Knox, who paid for all those suspiciously fresh corpses? He was not even called to give evidence at the trial. From the beginning, Knox claimed that he knew nothing of Burke and Hare's murders, and he bought corpses from them as he had from other resurrectionists. But the press and the Edinburgh mob thought differently; they went after him.

Normally, Knox's medical colleagues could have been expected to rise to his defense. But they didn't want to be associated with Burke and Hare, and they had never liked Knox, a stiff and arrogant man. They refused to defend him.

Knox believed that the whole incident would blow over in a short time, and he could then return to his highly successful career. Mobs howled around his house, but Knox was an old army surgeon, and was not afraid of violence. He carried a pistol and went about town protected by an escort of medical students.

For a while it appeared as if Knox's prediction that it would all blow over was accurate. After the scandal broke, attendance at his anatomy lectures actually went up. But the press would not let the case die.

Finally, Knox asked a group of ten respected gentlemen to make an impartial but private inquiry into his conduct. When this became known, it sparked a major riot. The inquiry continued anyway. In the end, the committee Knox himself appointed cleared him of legal responsibility, but the members did conclude he "had acted in a very incautious manner." The committee was particularly critical of Knox's instructions to his associates that they were to ask no questions of persons bringing in bodies that might tend to "diminish or divert the supply of subjects." Knox never admitted that he did anything wrong, but he did agree to be more careful in the future.

In the opinion of the public, however, Knox was just as guilty as Burke and Hare. A popular children's rhyme of the day ran:

> Down the close and up the stair,
> Round and round with Burke and Hare.
> Burke's the butcher, Hare's the thief,
> Knox's the man who buys the beef

Or another:

Hang Burke, banish Hare,
Burn Knox in Surgeon's Square

Knox was never burned, but he was shunned. Attendance at his anatomy classes dropped off sharply, until finally he could not attract enough students to keep teaching privately. No university would give him a post. They offered all manner of reasons for refusing him, never mentioning Burke and Hare, but that, of course, was what lay behind the refusals.

Ultimately, Knox was forced to leave Scotland altogether. He died in 1862, in London, at the age of seventy-two, a poor man but not a forgotten one. Long after his death, as the crimes of Burke and Hare were recounted in books, plays, and eventually films, Dr. Robert Knox was always featured as one of the villains.

Burke's execution and what followed was almost as grotesque as the crimes he committed. A crowd estimated at 25,000 men, women, and children gathered in the rain on January 27, 1829, to watch Burke hung on the gallows in Edinburgh's Landmarket. Though condemned men were often cheered by the mob that had come to see them die, Burke was no popular hero. He was hooted and jeered, and the crowd shouted that Hare and Knox should join him on the gallows.

After the hanging, the crowd surged forward to try to grab a souvenir, a piece of the hangman's rope or shavings from the murderer's coffin.

The next day Burke's corpse was to be dissected in the laboratory of Professor Alexander Monroe. Tickets to view the proceedings had been issued to leading citizens and a selected group of medical students. Hundreds of other medical students, who felt they were being cheated, staged a riot outside and broke the windows of the anatomical theater. The constables were called, but the crowd could not be calmed until it was agreed that students, in groups of fifty, were to be allowed inside.

After that, it was the turn of the general public. An estimated 30,000 people filed through the anatomical theater to see the corpse of the murderer. The writer, Sir Walter Scott, was appalled at the spectacle.

"The corpse of the murderer Burke is now lying in state at the College, in the anatomical class, and all the world flock to see him. Who is he that says we are not ill to please our subjects of curiosity? The strange means by which the wretch made his money are scarce more disgusting than the eager curiosity with which the public have licked up all the carrion details of this business."

There was a long line waiting outside the door of

the anatomical theater the next morning as well, but the professors decided to close down the show and get on with the dissection.

After the dissection, Burke's skeleton was reassembled and put on display at the Edinburgh University Medical School. It is still there today and still the object of much curious attention.

The era of body snatching in Scotland was drawing to a close. Partly in response to the Burke and Hare murders, laws were changed to allow anatomists more legal access to corpses. Once the profit was removed, the body snatchers faded away. But they left a legacy.

The Burke and Hare case was to become the basis for an excellent Robert Louis Stevenson short story called, appropriately, "The Body Snatcher." Wrote Stevenson:

"Somewhat as two vultures may swoop down upon a dying lamb, Fettes and MacFarlane [the body snatchers] were to be let loose upon the grave in that green and quiet resting place. The wife of a farmer, a woman who had lived for sixty years, and had been known for nothing but good butter and godly conversation, was to be rooted from her grave at midnight and carried, dead and naked, to that faraway city that she had always honored with her Sunday best; the place beside her family was to be empty till the crack of doom; her innocent and almost vulnerable members to be exposed to the last curiosity of the anatomist."

The story in turn became the basis for a low-budget, low-key yet compelling 1945 film, *The Body Snatcher*, starring Boris Karloff, with Bela Lugosi in a small but memorable role. This film was produced and written in part by Val Lewton, Hollywood's master of subtle horror. In 1959, the British remade the film with the title *The Flesh and the Fiends*, starring Peter Cushing. It was, as the title indicates, a bloodier version, but a far less effective one.

As late nineteenth-century London will always be associated with Jack the Ripper, early nineteenth-century Edinburgh will always be associated with the body snatchers, Burke and Hare.

8

▼ ▼

Dead but Not Buried

"Don't cry for me, Argentina"

Suddenly, because of the hit film *Evita*, Eva Perón is a hot topic again. And because of the genuinely bizarre and macabre circumstances surrounding not her life, but her death, she deserves a place in this book.

Eva Perón—Evita, as she was known—was the wife of Argentine dictator Juan Perón. She had been born poor and had become an actress and radio personality before she married Perón, an ambitious army man. Together, they were able to dominate Argentine politics for years during the late 1940s and early '50s. Evita was at least as popular as her husband and probably more so, particularly among the poor, who regarded her as their champion and very nearly a saint.

But Evita was stricken with cancer at the height of her power, and she died in 1952. She was only thirty-three years old. Even before her death, plans were being made to preserve her body with care that had not been seen since the days of the late pharaohs. Perón had already chosen an eminent Spanish mortician, Dr. Pedro Ara, to handle the embalming. Ara was a strange man. He kept a preserved head on the bar in his home, next to his bottles of wine. It was the excellent condition of this head that persuaded Perón that Ara was the man for the job of preserving his wife.

Ara hovered around the dying woman for weeks like a vulture, and the moment she breathed her last, he took possession of the corpse and began the embalming process. Before the process could really get started, the body was placed on display in a glass casket for two weeks. Millions of weeping Argentines viewed the corpse. Then the body was whisked off to a secret and specially built laboratory to which only Ara and Perón himself had the keys.

The final embalming process took over a year. In her best-selling biography of Eva Perón, Alicia Dujovne Ortez wrote, "The most profound secrecy would surround the long hours during which Evita would remain submerged in boiling pools of God knows what mysterious liquids."

Ara never revealed the process he used. Years later, when the corpse was once again being restored, the doctors said that the technique used was apparently the ancient method called "Spanish mummification." Preserving solutions were sent throughout the entire body. Parts were filled with wax, and the body was covered with a layer of hard wax. This gave it a waxy appearance, and led to the rumor that it was nothing more than a wax dummy.

Perón had plans to build a mausoleum of truly pharaonic proportions for the dead woman. It was to be three times the height of the Statue of Liberty. In the meantime, the body was kept under Ara's watchful eye, and from time to time wheeled out in its glass coffin to Perón rallies. Perón needed all the help he could get. Without a living Evita by his side, the dictator gradually lost popularity. In 1955, a military coup threw him out of power and into exile in Spain.

And what of Evita's mummy? It presented a tremendous problem for the new rulers of Argentina. It represented a potent symbol, around which supporters of the now-exiled dictator could rally, so they would have liked to be rid of it. But they couldn't just destroy the body. That would create too much popular resentment. For months they did nothing. They just left it in Ara's care. One military man who visited the secret laboratory described the corpse this way: "She was the size of a twelve-year-old girl. Her skin looked like wax, artificial. Her lips were painted red. If you tapped her finger it sounded hollow. Ara, the embalmer, did not part from it as if he loved it."

After months of hesitation, the military rulers came up with a plan that they called, very appropriately, "Operation Evasion." The body was taken at midnight from the secret laboratory to a military base where it was stored in a truck. But word leaked out and, mysteriously, flowers and candles appeared around the truck. So it was moved to another base, and then another. Always with the same results. At one point, the truck containing Evita's body was simply parked in downtown Buenos Aires. Again, the flowers and candles appeared. For the new rulers of Argentina, this was an intolerable and potentially dangerous situation.

At this point, the story becomes very murky. It seems that the body was stored for several years in the offices of the Information Service, inside a box marked "Radio Equipment." The guardian was now Colonel Carlos Eugenio Moori-Koening, chief of the army's Information Service. Moori-Koening appears to have fallen under the spell of the dead Evita. He was heard to mutter things like "She's mine. That woman is mine." He was ordered to bury the body in an obscure cemetery, but he failed to do so. He later claimed that he had already buried the body elsewhere. "I buried her standing up," he said. "Because she was a man." His superiors finally dismissed

Moori-Koening because they thought he had gone mad.

Finally, the military rulers decided that Evita could not be buried safely anywhere in Argentina, and the decision was made to send the body to Italy. In 1957, the preserved corpse was smuggled out of Argentina to Milan, where it was buried under the name Maria Maggi de Magistris, described as a "widow from Argentina." There it remained, in a plain grave for fourteen years. Very few knew where the body actually was, and the rumors flew. The most persistent rumor was that it had been taken to Rome, where it was being hidden in the Vatican under the special protection of the pope.

The political situation in Argentina had begun to change. Perón, who had been driven into exile, began to look better as the years passed. The myth of Perón, and particularly of Evita, continued to grow. There was a great demand to restore Evita's body to Perón. In truth, Juan Perón had never shown any great desire to have the body, but in 1971 it was finally located in the Milan cemetery and sent to him in Spain, whether he wanted it or not.

The body arrived at Perón's home hidden in a bakery truck. As with so much else in the bizarre tale, the details of what happened next are unclear and contradictory. According to some accounts, the body, aside from a bent ear and a few broken fingers, was in excellent shape. According to other accounts, however, the body had been mutilated, the head had practically been cut off, and the face appeared as if had been hit with a hammer. The damage, however, could be repaired.

At first, say some stories, Perón put the coffin in his dining room, where his third wife, Isabel, would sometimes talk to it during the meal. According to one genuinely macabre report, Isabel would brush and comb the cadaver's hair each morning, and sometimes lie on it to pick up energy from the dead woman.

Most of the time, however, Perón just kept the corpse in his attic. In 1973, Juan Perón returned in triumph to Argentina, where he once again became head of state. He talked about Evita, but he left her body back in Spain. By this time, Perón was an old and sick man. He died of a heart attack less than a year after his return, and was succeeded by his widow, Isabel.

Isabel recognized the weakness of her position and she brought Evita's body back to Argentina from the Perón attic in Madrid. Isabel tried to use Evita's body as an icon to boost her own fragile popularity. It worked for a while, but in 1976 Isabel Perón was overthrown in a military coup. The new rulers quietly turned Evita's corpse over to two of her sisters. Since then, she has been interred in the family crypt, protected by two trapdoors and three plates of steel. Only a small plaque announces her presence. The saga of the wandering corpse of Evita Perón is over —at least for now.

Evita Perón is not the only figure in history whose corpse has had difficulty finding a final resting place. The mummies of many of Egypt's greatest kings were moved, often many times, by pious priests trying to protect them from tomb robbers.

The corpse of Alexander the Great was stolen even before it was buried. Alexander died unexpectedly while campaigning in Asia in 353 B.C. In less than ten years, Alexander had conquered an enormous empire, but at his death he had no clear successors. Nor had he left any instructions as to where he wished to be buried. There was great rivalry among the conqueror's generals, who were in the process of carving up Alexander's empire among themselves, as to who would take custody of the corpse. Possession of the body of the conqueror would have been a unique status symbol, particularly since Alexander was regarded as a god by many of his soldiers.

It was decided that Alexander's body should be sent back to his homeland in Macedonia. But such an illustrious corpse could not travel in a simple wooden box. Alexander had to have a funeral chariot, the likes of which the world had never seen before.

Robin Lane Fox, in his biography, *Alexander the Great*, wrote:

"It [the corpse] was to lie among spices in a golden coffin with a gold lid, covered with purple embroidery on which rested Alexander's armour and famous Trojan shield; above it, a pillared canopy rose 36 feet high to a broad vault of gold and jewels, from which hung a curtain with rings and tassels and bells of warning; the cornice was carved with goats and stags and at each corner of the vault there were golden figures of Victory. . . . Paintings were attached to mesh netting down either side of the vault . . . gold lions guarded the coffin and a purple banner embroidered with an olive wreath was spread above the canopy's roof."

The whole elaborate contraption was to be drawn by sixty-four mules and had to be accompanied by a crew of engineers and road menders, to prepare the way. Building of the chariot took over two years, and by the time it was finished, those who were supposed to make sure it was sent to Macedonia were busy elsewhere. So Ptolemy, the general who had taken over the Egyptian part of Alexander's conquests, befriended the officer who had been left in charge of the funeral cortege. The chariot was secretly sent to Egypt, where Ptolemy put the coffin on display in Alexandria.

There it remained for centuries, becoming an object of pilgrimage for a whole series of would-be world conquerors. Alexander's body was probably destroyed in riots that ripped through Alexandria in the third century, though throughout history there have been occasional rumors that the remains of Alexander the Great were spirited away and hidden in some secret place, to await finders of a future age. The rumors are, alas, probably false.

As with Evita, political shifts often result in body shifts as well. Napoleon Bonaparte, who had once crowned himself emperor of the French, died in lonely exile on the island of Saint Helena in 1821, and was buried there. As the years passed, the hardships he had brought to France were forgotten. The glories of the Age of Napoleon appeared more glorious than ever in contrast to the drabness of nineteenth-century France.

Napoleon's ambitious nephew, Louis Napoleon, who was trying to use nostalgia as a means of rising to power, pushed hard to have his uncle's remains returned to Paris. The reigning king, Louis Philippe, held him off for a dozen years, but finally the pressure became too great, and the emperor's coffin was returned from St. Helena and installed in a magnificent tomb under the golden dome of the Invalides in Paris. It's still there.

The most politically significant body shift to take place in modern times involves the remains of the Soviet dictator, Joseph Stalin. Stalin died in 1953.

Upon his death, he was praised by his successors as a great leader and hero. His body was carefully embalmed and placed on permanent display next to that of V. I. Lenin, founder of the Soviet state, in a huge tomb in Moscow's Red Square. Lenin had died in 1924, and his remarkably well-preserved corpse has been on display since that time. Just what method of preservation was used remains a mystery; indeed, there have even been rumors that Lenin's body has long since been replaced by a wax figure, though no one knows for sure. Pedro Ara, the strange embalmer who preserved Evita Perón's corpse, was said by some to have been in charge of the preservation of Lenin. It was a story that Ara would neither confirm nor deny.

Placing Stalin's body next to that of Lenin was the highest possible honor the Soviet state could bestow. But Stalin's successors were not nearly as fond of him as their initial public statements indicated. Indeed, many regarded him as little short of a madman and a monster. Slowly, indications of a new attitude toward the dead leader began to leak out. In 1956, Nikita Khruschev and other leaders attacked Stalin openly at a Communist Party congress. Then, in 1961, the Soviet leaders decided to make the final symbolic move. The Lenin-Stalin mausoleum was "closed for repairs." When it reopened, Lenin's remains were once again on display in solitary splender.

Stalin's body had been quietly removed to a modest grave in a cemetery near the Kremlin wall.

Though the Communist state has fallen, Lenin's well-preserved corpse (or a wax replica) is still on display for the faithful at the great mausoleum in Red Square.

How long it will remain there in the turbulent conditions of the new Russia is anybody's guess.

Back from the Dead
TEN CLASSIC FILMS

The theme of raising the dead has been central to some of the finest horror films ever made—no, let's expand that to some of the finest films ever made, period. Here are ten of my favorites, in no particular order. And every one of these films is available on videotape.

1. FRANKENSTEIN (1931). Directed by James Whale. Starring Boris Karloff, Colin Clive, Mae Clarke, Edward van Sloan, Dwight Frye, Lionel Belmore. One of Universal Pictures' cycle of great horror films, and probably the definitive monster movie. Jack Pierce's makeup for Karloff fixed our image of the monster forever. Don't overlook Dwight Frye's wonderful turn as the crazed assistant.

2. BRIDE OF FRANKENSTEIN (1935). Directed by James Whale. Starring Boris Karloff, Colin Clive, Elsa Lanchester, Ernest Thesiger, Valerie Hobson, Dwight Frye, John Carradine, Una O'Connor. That rarity, a sequel that is better than the original, and in the view of many fans (including this one) the finest horror film ever made. There is a rich vein of dry wit that runs through the chills, and keeps the film from ever feeling dated. It is sometimes shown without the Mary Shelley prologue—which is a shame.

3. SON OF FRANKENSTEIN (1939). Directed by Rowland V. Lee. Starring Boris Karloff, Basil Rathbone, Lionel Atwill, Josephine Hutchinson, Bela Lugosi, Emma Dunn. Universal did it again. Even without director James Whale, this third in the Frankenstein series is still a winner. Karloff, in his last serious outing as the monster is almost overshadowed by Lugosi as the deformed assistant, Ygor, and Atwell's wooden-armed police chief. It's a little creaky with age, and you'll laugh at parts that weren't supposed to be funny. But it's still well worth seeing.

4. MARY SHELLEY'S FRANKENSTEIN (1994). Directed by Kenneth Branagh. Starring Kenneth Branagh, Robert De Niro, Tom Hulce, Helena Bonham Carter, Aidan Quinn, Ian Holm, Richard Briers, John Cleese. Given that Branagh is today's most brilliant actor/director, and the rest of the cast is truly stellar, this film should have been better. But it is not the disaster many critics declared it to be. With its gorgeously gothic look and feel, it is far closer to Mary Shelley's novel than anything put on the screen. Critic Leonard Maltin complained, "And what's with the story framing with sea captain Quinn." It's in the book, but as I said, nobody reads the book anymore. Forget the critics and grab this one on video.

5. YOUNG FRANKENSTEIN (1974). Director Mel Brooks. Starring Gene Wilder, Marty Feldman, Madeline Kahn, Peter Boyle, Teri Garr, Cloris Leachman, Kenneth Mars, Richard Hadyn, Gene Hackman. Parodies of horror films are easy to make. Too easy, and more often than not they fall flat. Not this one. It is, bar none, the best horror film parody ever made, and Mel Brooks' funniest film. Everyone has a favorite moment in this film. Mine is Dr. Frankenstein and his monster singing and tap-dancing to "Puttin' on the Ritz." Filmed in glorious black-and-white, a rarity in 1974.

6. THE MUMMY (1932). Directed by Karl Freund. Starring Boris Karloff, Zita Johann, David Manners, Edward Van Sloan. Ignore the story, which is pretty silly, and concentrate on the atmosphere, and a superb performance by Karloff, and you will find this film a truly wonderful fantasy. The scene where the mummy comes back to life and "takes a little walk" is one of the most memorable of all horror films.

7. THE MUMMY'S HAND (1940). Directed by Christy Cabanne. Starring Dick Foran, Wallace Ford, Peggy Moran, George Zucco, Tom Tyler, Eduardo Ciannelli. This is a semi-sequel to the 1932 Karloff classic, but without Karloff, and it's nowhere near as good. But it is the first of the "Kharis" films, in which the now familiar bandage-swathed lumbering corpse appears throughout the whole film. It starts off almost as a comedy, but by the end it's pretty scary.

8. THE BODY SNATCHER (1945). Directed by Robert Wise. Starring Boris Karloff, Henry Daniell, Bela Lugosi, Edith Atwater, Russell Wade. In 1942, RKO Studios put writer Val Lewton in charge of a special production unit formed to turn out low-budget horror films. The result was a series of minor classics of which this adaptation of the Robert Louis

Stevenson story, based on the Burke and Hare murders, is probably the best. This is a film for the true horror film buff. Devotees of chain-saw films will find it slow.

9. WHITE ZOMBIE (1932). Directed by Victor Halperin. Starring Bela Lugosi, Madge Bellamy, Joseph Cawthorn, Robert Frazer. Lugosi plays Murder Legendre, an evil sorcerer in this first ever film about reanimated corpses in Haiti. Universal Pictures lent its makeup genius, Jack Pierce, to United Artists to create Lugosi's memorable satanic makeup. Lugosi attempting a French accent, over his already heavily Hungarian accented English, sounds absolutely bizarre. The film is old-fashioned and stilted, but it has a weird dreamlike quality. It was very popular when first released, and though rarely seen today it is still very much worth a look.

10. NIGHT OF THE LIVING DEAD (1968). Directed by George A. Romero. Starring Duane Jones, Judith O'Dea, Russell Streiner, Karl Hardman, Keith Wayne. Independently produced on a shoestring budget, it has been described as "the best film ever made in Pittsburgh." It's lots better than that. Romero's vision of flesh-eating zombies touched a nerve, and instead of falling into oblivion, which is the fate of most pictures of this type, it became a cult favorite and spawned an entire generation of similar and usually inferior imitations. Considered shockingly gruesome in its day, it is not gory by today's standards, but it is scary by any standards.

SELECTED BIBLIOGRAPHY

ADAMS, DOUGLAS. *Dead and Buried?*. New York: Bell, 1972.

ASHE, GEOFFREY, et al. *The Quest for Arthur's Britain*. London: Granada, 1982.

BOJARSKI, RICHARD. *The Films of Bela Lugosi*. Secaucus, NJ: Citadel, 1980.

————— and KENNETH BEALE. *The Films of Boris Karloff*. Secaucus, NJ: Citadel, 1978.

CAVENDISH, RICHARD. *King Arthur and the Grail: The Arthurian Legends and Their Meaning*. New York: Taplinger, 1979.

COHEN, DANIEL. *The Body Snatchers*. Philadelphia: Lippincott, 1975.

—————. *Voodoo, Devils, and the New Invisible World*. New York: Dodd, Mead, 1972.

COHN, NORMAN. *The Pursuit of the Millennium* (rev.ed.). New York: Oxford University Press, 1970.

COLE, HUBERT. *Things for the Surgeon*. London: William Heinemann, 1964.

DAVIS, WADE. *The Serpent and the Rainbow*. New York: Simon and Schuster, 1985.

DE GIVRY, GRILLOT. *Witchcraft, Magic and Alchemy*. New York: Dover, 1971.

DESROCHES-NOBLECOURT, CHRISTINE. *Tutankhamon*. Greenwich, CT: New York Graphic Society, 1963.

DOUGLAS, DRAKE. *Horrors*. London: John Baker, 1967.

EL MAHDY, CHRISTINE. *Mummies, Myth and Magic*. New York: Thames and Hudson, 1989.

FARSON, DANIEL. *Vampires, Zombies, and Monster Men*. New York: Doubleday, 1976.

FLORESCU, RADU. *In Search of Frankenstein*. Boston: New York Graphic Society, 1975.

GLUT, DONALD. *The Frankenstein Legend: A Tribute to Mary Shelley and Boris Karloff*. Metuchen, NJ: The Scarecrow Press, 1973.

HURSTON, ZORA NEALE. *Tell My Horse*. Philadelphia: Lippincott, 1938.

HUXLEY, FRANCIS. *The Invisibles: Voodoo Gods of Haiti*. New York: McGraw-Hill, 1969.

LACY, NORRIS J. (ed.). *The Arthurian Encyclopedia*. New York: Peter Bedrick Books, 1986.

ORTEZ, ALICIA DUJOUNE. *Eva Perón*. New York: St. Martins, 1996.

ROUGHEAD, WILLIAM. *Burke and Hare, Notable British Trials*. London: William Hodge, 1948.

SHELLEY, MARY. *The Annotated Frankenstein.* New York: Clarkson N. Potter, 1977.

TIME-LIFE BOOKS (ed.). *The Fall of Camelot.* Alexandria, VA: Time-Life Books, 1986.

————. *Legends of Valor.* Alexandria, VA: Time-Life Books, 1984.

————. *The Secret Arts.* Alexandria, VA: Time-Life Books, 1987.

WILSON, COLIN and DAMON WILSON. *Unsolved Mysteries.* New York: Galahad Books, 1992.